Sam couldn't

It had nothing to do filled with worry for her son, or the way she'd cried out while she was injured. No sirree. She was trouble, and he wanted nothing to do with her.

But against his better judgment, something about Rachel Walker drew him like a moth to a flame. By midday, word would spread all over town that a new woman was moving into Finnegan's Valley. No doubt she'd draw attention from every bachelor for miles around.

Not him. He didn't have time to notice a pretty woman. He'd accepted his fate as a confirmed bachelor long ago. He'd had his chance at love and ruined it. But deep down inside, he still couldn't help yearning for a family of his own.

Someone to shower his life upon. Someone all his own who loved him in return no matter what.

With Rachel in his life, somehow he sensed he would never be the same again.

Books by Leigh Bale

Love Inspired

The Healing Place
The Forever Family

LEIGH BALE

is a multiple award-winning author of inspirational and romantic fiction. In 2006, Leigh won the RWA's prestigious Golden Heart Award and sold her first book to Steeple Hill Books' Love Inspired line. A member of Phi Kappa Phi Honor society, Leigh also belongs to various chapters of RWA, including the Sacramento Valley Rose; the Faith, Hope and Love Chapter; the Hearts through History Romance Writers; and the Golden Network. She is the mother of two and lives in Nevada with her professor husband of twenty-seven years. When she isn't working or writing, Leigh loves playing with her beautiful granddaughter, serving in her church congregation and taking classes to finish her graduate degree. Visit her Web site at www.LeighBale.com.

The Forever Family
Leigh Bale

Steeple
Hill®

Published by Steeple Hill Books™

STEEPLE HILL BOOKS

Steeple
Hill®

Recycling programs
for this product may
not exist in your area.

ISBN-13: 978-0-373-87546-7

THE FOREVER FAMILY

Copyright © 2009 by Lora Lee Bale

Printed in U.S.A.

In God is my salvation and my glory: the rock of my strength, and my refuge, is in God. Trust in him at all times; ye people, pour out your heart before him: God is a refuge for us.

—*Psalms* 62:7–8

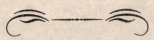

This book is dedicated to my dear Aunt Shirley,
the bravest fighter in the ring.

And many thanks to Dr. David Baggett, DVM,
for answering my veterinarian questions.
To Chris Platt, the best critique partner a girl
could ever ask for. To Melissa Endlich, for
believing in me. And to Dan Baird. Thanks, Dad.

Chapter One

Rachel Walker blinked her eyes, which were gritty with fatigue. Exhaustion burned through her body, but she fought it off. She had to stay awake. Had to focus on the dark road. The window defroster had stopped working fifteen miles outside of Finley, Nevada.

She peered at the clock on the dashboard. Two thirty-five in the morning. Just a few more miles and she could sleep.

A shiver trembled over her body and she tightened her frozen fingers around the steering wheel of her blue 1984 compact car. Her breath made little puffs each time she exhaled. Without heat, the windshield kept fogging over. She rubbed her gloved hand in a circular spot on the glass pane so she could see out.

Heavy snow blanketed the car, falling from the night sky in thick, wet dollops. With no more than forty feet of visibility in front of her, she slowed to a crawl. She should have stopped at the last town instead of going on in this blizzard, but she didn't have a lot of money for a motel, and she needed to make her cash last as long as possible.

Dread swept her when she thought of the impending

holiday season. Without any family around, baking a turkey, pies and rolls for Thanksgiving dinner wouldn't be much fun. And then Christmas.

Even worse.

Though she still mourned her husband, she had to think of Danny and try to build happy memories for him. After losing his father ten months earlier, he sure needed something joyful in his life. She glanced in the rearview mirror at her seven-year-old son sleeping in the backseat. She smiled as she gazed at his sweet face. So trusting, so serene.

A thatch of blond hair peeked out from beneath Danny's red knit cap. Blond like his father, with dazzling blue eyes, an impish nose and a mischievous smile that melted her heart.

The top of Danny's seat belt slanted across his small body. With these horrible road conditions, she'd insisted he wear it before she bundled a heavy quilt around him. He obeyed begrudgingly, hunched against the teddy bear stuffed between his head and the cold door. She wished she dared let him remove the seat belt and lie down. He'd be more comfortable, but it wouldn't be safe.

He shivered. With the heater inoperable, they both wore thick winter coats. Soon, they'd be at their new home and could get warm. Soon, they'd be safe.

An occasional glimpse of the tops of the guardrails kept Rachel from driving off the road into the snowy embankment. She'd never felt more alone than right now.

Please, God. Please keep us safe tonight.

The last time she came to see Grammy, Alex had been driving. They'd passed through Nevada just over a year ago, heading for the sunny beaches of California to enjoy a short vacation. She'd invited Grammy to come along, but the elderly lady refused. Within two months, Alex had died of a brain aneurysm, taking her heart with him—

Enough of that! The memory of her beloved husband brought tears to her eyes and she brushed them away. She could barely see out the window already. The year since Alex's death had been followed by a long struggle to make ends meet. When she received the call last month that Grammy had died quietly in her sleep, Rachel decided to move west. Grammy had left her old farmhouse to Rachel, and she intended to live there with Danny and start a new life.

The rhythmic *thwack*ing of the windshield wipers brought her comfort. The wheels of the small travel trailer she pulled behind her car thumped through the heavy snow. The trailer contained her worldly possessions: bedding, clothes, picture albums, Danny's toys, and the oak rocking chair Alex presented to her the day they brought Danny home from the hospital. Her grandmother's house contained all the furniture they would need. She had enough money to get them settled and then she'd find a job. They'd make do or do without.

Four more miles. In this storm, she might get lost or stuck in the snow if she tried going out to Grammy's house along the dark country roads. Maybe she'd get a cheap motel room after all, just for tonight. She'd drive out to Grammy's place in the morning, once the snowplows had time to do their work. The house hadn't been occupied since Grammy died. It had a solid roof, but Rachel figured the place would need a thorough cleaning.

As she entered the outskirts of town, several small billboards appeared on her right, listing various services, clubs and churches in the community. Through the falling snow, Rachel couldn't make out any names. Again, she rubbed at the windshield to clear a spot to see, longing for friends. Wanting to belong. Maybe she could get involved in her new community.

Driving down Main Street, she scanned the dim lights of the bank, diner and drugstore. Everything closed. Good thing they'd stopped earlier for a hamburger and fries in Eureka. The haze of streetlights gleamed eerily in the falling snow, not another soul in sight.

Just ahead, she made out the large yellow sign of a Best Homestyle motel; the only one in town. Clean and inexpensive. Relief flooded her fatigued body. Sleep seemed a treasured dream about to become a reality.

The windshield wipers stopped dead in midswing. Rachel gasped and flipped the lever back and forth, desperate to clear the heavy snowflakes from her view.

"Please don't stop now. Just one more mile," she whispered, trying to get the wipers to work.

A prayer for help rose to her lips just as the red stoplight appeared out of nowhere. As she crossed the intersection, she slammed on the brakes. The car surged forward, sliding on black ice. The trailer jackknifed. Terror shot up her spine and she spun the steering wheel, trying to regain control of the car. The trailer groaned, then slammed against the car, wrenching Rachel's head to one side. An enormous shape appeared out of nowhere. Oncoming headlights blinded her as a large, white truck loomed into her path.

"No!"

The cry tore from her constricted throat. The car and trailer squealed, careening into the other lane. As the other vehicle struck her car, her ears filled with the horrible sound of crunching metal and shattering glass. Danny's frightened scream filled the air. Pain shot through her left side. The impact caused her head to flip forward like a rag doll and smack the steering wheel. It happened so fast, yet everything moved in slow motion. One thought pounded her brain.

Danny! Wearing his seat belt. In the backseat. Away from the collision.

Her heart thudded as the car came to a jerking stop. She

sat with her nose pressed against the car door, her seat belt biting into her shoulder. When she tried to move, a shot of pain flashed through her head and arm. Her body felt bruised.

Broken.

A thin whimper came from the backseat. She clawed at the door handle. She had to check Danny. Had to make certain he was okay.

The door opened, and snowflakes fell from the sky like wet confetti on New Year's Eve. She lifted her head, staring into a wind tunnel of white, trying to clear her vision. Trying to focus on the man's face materializing in front of her.

"Hey, lady, you okay?"

Her tongue felt like a chunk of wood and she couldn't speak. She reached her hand toward the man, mumbling her concern for her son. Begging this stranger to help her. Knives of pain sliced through her left arm. She inhaled sharply, fighting off the dizzying stars that seemed to spot her vision. Her eyelids slid closed and everything went black.

"She's awake, Doctor."

Rachel blinked her eyes, feeling disoriented as she stared into a bright light pointed at her pupils. She clenched her eyes shut, her mind spinning. She tried to sort out what had happened.

"Danny!" she croaked, trying to sit up.

Firm hands pressed her down. "Easy, now. Just lie still for a moment."

A man's voice reached her consciousness, soft and soothing.

"Alex?" she whispered, forcing herself to open her eyes. She choked back a hoarse cry as pain pierced her brain.

No, this man wasn't her husband. Too handsome, his hair and eyes too dark. His brow furrowed as his gaze focused on her face.

"My son…where is he?" she asked.

"He's fine. Good thing you wore your seat belts. It saved your lives."

"I want to see him," she insisted. She had to know Danny was safe. Had to see him for herself.

"I'll get him." A woman's voice, then retreating footsteps echoed down a hallway, but soon returned. A rustling of movement sounded beside her.

"Mommy!"

She opened her eyes and found Danny's sweet face nearby. The boy leaned across the bed—no, a cot pushed against the wall of what appeared to be a storage room. The smell of antiseptic filled the air. Candles sat on the nearby table, their flames flickering in the shadows. The storm must have thrown the power out. Shelves lined the opposite wall filled with sample-sized bags of dog and cat food and boxes of medical supplies.

Where was she? The town of Finley didn't have a hospital, or even a clinic. Maybe she'd been taken to Elko, over one hundred miles away. But they couldn't get her through the snowstorm, could they?

Danny's brows scrunched together with concern. "Mommy?"

"Oh, honey. Are you okay?" She tried to reach for him, but pain shot through her left arm. She lay still, wishing she could hold him in her arms.

"I'm fine, but you don't look too good. Your head's bleedin' again."

"It is?" She brushed her fingers across her forehead, feeling a large bump and a butterfly bandage someone had put there. No wonder her head throbbed.

"Are you gonna die?" His mouth puckered as if he might cry.

"No, of course not, baby. I'll be fine. You're sure you're all right?"

"Yeah, look what Gladys gave me."

Who was Gladys?

Danny stuck a red lollipop in front of Rachel's eyes. Focusing made her stomach churn. In her hazy vision, she could make out the doctor and a woman standing behind Danny, both wearing blue smocks. A stethoscope dangled from the man's neck beside a name badge that read: Dr. Sam. He leaned close to Danny and smiled, showing a dimple in his left cheek. "All right, son, why don't you go with Gladys, now? She'll get you something to eat and put you to bed. We'll take good care of your mommy."

"Okay." Danny slid away.

Rachel reached for him, feeling a sinking of dread. Her fingers grasped air. "Where...where are you taking my son?"

The doctor spoke close by. "Gladys lives just down the street. Danny can bunk in with her son, Charlie."

"Charlie?"

"Yeah, the two boys are the same age. Don't worry. He'll be fine. I'll take you there just as soon as you feel well enough to walk."

Rachel relaxed for a moment, then reconsidered. "Am I going to be okay?"

In the vague light, she could make out the doctor's frown and intelligent brown eyes. A thatch of hair the color of a crow's wing fell over his high forehead. He brushed his hand across the raspy stubble on his chin and his brows gathered together in perplexity. "Of course. You just need rest."

Good. Danny needed her now more than ever.

She felt the doctor's hand against her shoulder, warm and comforting. How she missed her husband. How she missed his firm, take-charge manner. Thinking about Alex caused tears to bead in the corners of her eyes.

The doctor patted her hand and placed it beneath the thick quilt covering her. She allowed her body to relax.

"Take it easy. You're safe now," the doctor said.

Buoyed by his words, she tried to think good thoughts. Somewhere in her imagination, a dog barked, followed by the bleating of a sheep.

A sheep? She must be dreaming.

"Oh," she groaned. If only this muzzy feeling would vacate her brain, she'd be able to think clearly.

She listened to the woman's muted tones as she spoke to the doctor, aware of their presence in the room but unable to make out their words. She tried to focus, but her insides felt jittery. "Can you give me something for the pain?"

"Sure. What would you like?"

How odd. Shouldn't the doctor know what to give her in a situation like this? "My arm and head hurts."

She opened her eyes and peered at the man standing beside the door. She recognized his stance. Legs braced. One hand cocked on his hip. Gaze piercing her to the bone. The kind of man who knew how to handle himself and never backed away from a fight. In the depths of his eyes, she saw a shadow of frustration. She couldn't blame him. It was the middle of the night after all. No doubt he resented her for disturbing his sleep.

He leaned one hip against the counter and spoke to the cabinets as he picked up a bottle of pills and popped the lid. He shook several white tablets onto the palm of his hand. "Your arm has a bad sprain and you'll have a nasty bruise, but nothing's broken. I think you might have a concussion, so we'll keep an eye on you for a few more hours. I don't have any powerful medications for humans. Will some aspirin suffice?"

She looked away. A patchwork quilt draped her body. Definitely not normal hospital issue. She expected white sheets and a sterile blanket. "Aspirin is fine."

He brought her a paper cup with water and watched as she took it and swallowed the pills down. She handed the empty cup back to him and he balled it up and tossed it at the garbage can, where it made a perfect two-point shot.

"What kind of doctor are you?"

"I'm a veterinarian."

She laughed, her mind whirling as she flung back the quilt to free her legs. Still dressed in her jeans and heavy blue sweater, she wriggled her bare toes. Someone had removed her socks and shoes. The doctor or Gladys? It made her feel odd to think of a strange man handling her bare feet. "You're kidding."

"Afraid not." He gave her a look that told her he was serious. He pointed at her shoes sitting beside the bed, and she swung her legs over the side of the cot. Her feet rested against the cold linoleum floor, helping her feel grounded. From the outer room, she caught the distinct sound of a cat meowing.

She stared at the collar of his denim shirt, listening to the deep timbre of his voice. "Doctor Greene's out of town until Wednesday. If we weren't in the middle of a blizzard, Lloyd would have driven you to Elko for X-rays. Instead, he brought you here to me."

"Lloyd?"

"He's the local law-enforcement here in Finley. Carl called him after you hit his truck."

Her head kept spinning. "Who is Carl?"

"Carl Frasier, the driver of the truck you hit with your car." He sounded slightly annoyed at having to repeat himself.

Of course! She remembered the accident with frightening clarity. "I'm sorry you had to come out in the middle of the night to help Danny and me."

He didn't respond and a swelling silence followed.

"Where…where are my car and belongings?" she asked.

"The accident totaled your car. Lloyd towed your trailer over to Gladys's house. It's intact, but the contents are a mess."

Great! No transportation and no money to buy a decent car.

Thankfully, she still had collision insurance. Too bad she'd sold Grammy's old sedan when she came in for the funeral. She only got five hundred dollars for the junker and used the money to buy a travel trailer. How was she going to get to Grammy's place, five miles outside of town? She prayed nothing else went wrong.

She struggled to stand and instantly regretted it. Her legs wobbled and she feared her knees might buckle. Nausea settled in her stomach. A jolt of pain swept her arm, leaving her weak and shaking. As she sat down, she bit back a groan, wishing she could sleep for a few hours. But she had to think of Danny. Had to find out how serious her predicament was.

"Easy there," the doctor urged, as he reached to help her up. Once she found her bearings, he withdrew quickly, as if touching her burned his fingers.

His gaze swept her forearms where a myriad of pink and purple scars covered the smooth flesh. She jerked her sleeves down to hide the ugliness; a constant reminder of why she feared and hated dogs. And why she usually wore long sleeves.

"Do they hurt?" he asked.

She almost flinched, wishing he hadn't noticed her scars. Shaking her head, she leaned against the wall and clenched her eyes closed, willing her insides to settle. "No, they're old wounds I prefer to forget. Where am I?"

"You're in my medical office," he said.

She swayed, her hands shaking.

"You sure you feel like sitting up?" He stood beside her, all broad shoulders and narrow hips, wearing faded blue jeans and scuffed cowboy boots. Rachel wasn't surprised by his attire. Not in this ranching town. Tall, lean and ruggedly handsome. The complete opposite of Alex, who'd been only five feet eight inches tall, always wore an Oxford shirt and ties even on Saturdays, and had a slight paunch. It never mattered to Rachel. Alex would always be the love of her life. From the first day they met, he'd been the kindest, gentlest man she ever knew. A good provider and fiercely protective of her and Danny. Ah, how she missed him.

"I'm fine."

"Okay, but take it slow."

She reached for her socks. "You mean to tell me this Lloyd person brought me to a *vet* for medical assistance?"

No doubt her shrill voice sounded ungrateful.

"With a blizzard and Doc Greene out of town, Lloyd figured I was the next best thing." Lloyd had probably dragged the doctor out of bed in the middle of the night to help her.

She pulled her tennis shoes on and tied them, trying to sort out everything. Finley had only one small grocery store in town, no movie theater and one family-owned diner where they served the best steak fries she'd ever eaten. Claridge's Diner. Maybe they needed a waitress.

Grammy used to drive almost two hours to the nearest dentist and hospital in Elko. The only medical doctor in Finley had retired from Los Angeles ten years earlier and opened a two-room clinic on Mondays and for emergencies. What more could you expect from a ranching community with less than three thousand people?

The window rattled with a gust of wind. Rachel flinched and stared at the door. She was jumpy as a frog.

"Who are you?" she asked.

"Sam Thorne." The doctor held out a hand and she shook it, feeling the gruff calluses on his palm. Strong hands, capable of mending fence and riding wild horses. The complete opposite of Alex and his soft accountant's hands.

"And who are you?" He lifted one brow, showing a hint of amusement. Yet his quirked smile showed only friendliness.

"I'm Rachel Walker. I guess I'm lucky Finley has a vet. Thanks for helping us."

"You're welcome." Dr. Thorne gave half a smile, showing that dimple in his cheek. He appeared to be in his midthirties, maybe seven or eight years older than her. His face looked rustic and too gruff, his chin too blunt. He had a nice mouth and a devil-may-care smile that should send any sensible girl running in the opposite direction. So why did she smile back?

His expression faded and he turned away, replacing the lid on a bottle of hydrogen peroxide before tossing soiled gauze into the trash can. "Where were you headed before the accident?"

"Here. I own a farmhouse in Finnegan's Valley. Danny and I plan to live there."

His eyebrows drew together and he frowned. "The old Duarte place is the only farmhouse out there."

"Yes, Myra Duarte was my grandmother. She left the house to me when she died six weeks ago."

He gave a low whistle. "Well, I'll be. You're Myra's granddaughter."

A statement, not a question.

"You knew my grandmother?"

"And your grandfather. When I was young, I bucked hay for Frank Duarte during the summer months to help pay my college tuition. Sad thing, losing Myra. She made the best watermelon pickles in five counties. She used to take after me with a broom whenever Craig Seeley and I raided her apple orchard."

That sounded like Grammy. Ask her nice, and Myra Duarte would give you her last crust of bread. But steal from her, and watch out!

Talking about her grandparents made Rachel feel warm and nostalgic. How she missed their generosity and quiet strength. They never had much, but they always opened their home to her during the summer months when she was a kid.

Dr. Thorne studied her face. "I seem to remember you bouncing around in pigtails when you came to visit as a child."

Rachel studied the doctor. A foggy recollection filled her mind of a young, handsome man wearing a scruffy cowboy hat as he worked the fields with the other hands Grandpa hired each summer. Back then, Sam Thorne had been too old to pay much attention to Frank Duarte's little granddaughter from back east. And she'd been too young to care about anything more than swimming in the pond and trying out the new shade of nail polish Grammy bought for her at Granger's General Store. Her grandfather died almost ten years ago, and she had no other family. They'd be content in Finley. Nothing else mattered.

Dr. Thorne tossed a quick glance her way, his ears reddening. He seemed embarrassed by her close scrutiny as he dropped a small pair of scissors into a sterile jar of green fluid. "We'll be neighbors. I live about half a mile east of your place."

"So, you're the one who bought my grandparent's farmland a few years ago."

"Yes, I built a house and barn in Finnegan's Valley. Someday, I hope to build a large animal hospital out there."

"I remember Grammy telling me all about it in her letters. I saw your place when I came in for her burial."

A doctor in Elko had called to let Rachel know Grammy had died. Rachel never even got to say goodbye, although she had told Grammy often over the phone and in letters that she loved her.

Dr. Thorne took a deep breath and let it go. "After Frank died, Myra received quite a bit of money from the sale of her land. I'm sure she left you well set for life."

Her head pounded like a sledgehammer. "I was her heir, but I only received the house."

His brow furrowed with doubt. "Then who got the money?"

"There was none. Grammy had no bank accounts. She always paid her bills in cash."

That was so like Grammy. Knowing she was dying, she had settled her obligations beforehand. Tears burned the backs of Rachel's eyes. How she wished she'd been here when Grammy died.

"Come on. I'll take you over to Gladys's house where you can get some sleep." Although he reached to help her, she sensed his detachment. Even though he spoke with fondness for her grandparents, he seemed ill at ease with her. They'd gotten off to a bad start and she wasn't certain why.

"You came all the way from Finnegan's Valley in this storm just to help me?"

He shook his head. "I was already here. I came into town earlier to eat supper with Gladys and Charlie and I couldn't get home because of the blizzard."

Ah, Dr. Thorne must have a thing for Gladys. Surprising, considering Gladys looked older than Sam by at least six years. Maybe in a small town like Finley, the pickings were slim.

He snorted, as if reading her thoughts. "Gladys is my older sister and Charlie's my nephew."

"Oh." A flush of embarrassment heated Rachel's face.

As he took her arm, she felt the strength in his big, solid hand. The electricity came back on, flooding the office with light. Rachel blinked her eyes and breathed a sigh of relief. Somehow with the lights on, the doctor didn't seem as threatening or her situation quite so bleak.

"That's a good sign." Dr. Thorne blew out the candles before he stepped to the door and disappeared from view.

"Wait!" Rachel called, unable to explain the panic rising in her throat.

Dr. Thorne returned with her coat. "I'm not leaving you."

She breathed a deep sigh and nodded, trying to calm down.

Still, she couldn't shake a feeling of unease. She didn't want to impose on the doctor, and yet she didn't want to be alone either. She felt caught in the middle of her own emotions.

When Dr. Thorne handed her the coat, he stood close to her. Too close. Rachel took the garment, then stepped away.

Chapter Two

Sam watched as Rachel Walker struggled to put her coat on over her sprained arm. When she flinched, he lifted the weight of the garment so she could slip it on. She smiled her thanks, fumbling with the zipper.

A lock of blond hair fell across her eyes and she tucked it back behind her ear. With her manicured nails, dainty features and soft hands, she reminded him too much of Melanie. He could spot a city girl from a mile away. It didn't matter that she was Frank and Myra Duarte's granddaughter. He doubted this woman had ever worked a hard day in her life.

No, siree. He wanted nothing to do with her.

He stood back, feeling surly. Against his better judgment, something about Rachel Walker drew him like a moth to flame. By midday, word would spread all over town that a new woman was moving into Finnegan's Valley, just south of town. No doubt she'd draw attention from every bachelor for miles around.

Not him. Not only was he too old for her, but he didn't have time for a pretty young woman who demanded lots of attention. Love passed him by long ago. He'd had his chance and ruined it. He accepted that. But he still couldn't help yearning for a family of his own. He had Gladys and Charlie, but it wasn't the same.

As he walked to the front door, he felt Rachel's eyes boring into him like a drill. When he turned, he found her checking her wristwatch. "What time is it? My watch must have been damaged during the crash."

"Just after four a.m. Almost time to get up. I may have to take a snowmobile out to my place to feed the livestock."

"Do you have a lot of animals out at your place?"

He didn't even crack a smile. "You could say that. Twenty-three head of cattle, eight horses, five cats, three pigs, two dogs and a new litter of pups born last week. I fed them before I left last night, but they'll go hungry if I'm not back in time to feed them and break the ice over their watering troughs."

She gave a short laugh. "I can't imagine caring for that many animals. I killed Danny's goldfish when I forgot to feed the poor thing for three days. Danny still hasn't forgiven me. What he really wants is a dog."

Yeah, she looked like the goldfish type. Probably didn't do well with live plants, either.

She clamped her mouth shut, as if realizing she'd told him too much. He didn't speak as they walked past the kennels to the front office. A tabby cat lay curled in its cage, watching them with glowing eyes. A dog stood and stretched lazily before giving a shrill bark. Rachel jumped, her eyes widening with fear.

"It's okay. They won't bother you," he assured her.

"Are they sick?" she asked.

"Nah, they're just boarding with me while their owners are out of town. Gladys and Charlie feed and play with them a couple times each day. Gladys is a trained vet tech and works for me."

"Oh, and what does a vet tech do?"

"Basically, she's my assistant," he explained.

"Oh."

He left her standing in the front office while he locked the back door. When he joined her again, he caught her staring at a sign in his front window that read: Help Wanted—Receptionist. Inquire inside.

Great! Now she'd ask for the job. She obviously needed an income. He didn't know why, but he didn't want to hire her. She couldn't be worse than the last receptionist he'd hired, but something about this woman put him on edge. She made him feel strange and out of sorts.

He discouraged further conversation by flicking off the light and opening the front door. A blast of wind and snow struck them, rattling the front windows. Rachel gasped. Her first step outside, the rubber soles of her impractical tennis shoes slipped against the icy pavement. She cried out and grabbed for his arm, and he found himself holding on to her so she wouldn't fall. In the dim shadows of the street light, she stared up into his eyes, her mouth rounding with surprise.

Sam didn't smile, but his heart rate sped up. He cleared his voice as he clasped her elbow. "Sorry, ma'am. I should've taken your arm."

"It's okay." She spoke above the roar of the storm, flashing him a forgiving smile that melted his frozen heart.

He knew then he'd crossed an invisible threshold he didn't understand. As he sheltered her from the brunt of the storm with his own body, he realized he couldn't go back in time and sensed he would never be the same again.

Hunching her shoulders against the wind, Rachel shuffled through the snow down the dark street. She was highly conscious of the strong man walking beside her, holding onto her arm. The cold and wet beat against her, stealing her breath. She could barely see in front of her feet, but Dr. Thorne seemed to know the way. His presence comforted her for some odd reason.

By the time they reached Gladys's house, Rachel's ears, feet, hands and nose felt numb with cold. Snowflakes wet her face and she brushed them away. Her hair felt weighted down with dampness.

Dr. Thorne led Rachel to the back porch, where he immediately released her arm. In the darkness of the storm, she could just make out the color of blue trim around the shutters. He opened the screen door, and she brushed off her coat before preceding him inside. Warmth engulfed her, and she caught the tantalizing scent of cinnamon. A night-light by the kitchen sink gleamed red across the refrigerator, table, four chairs, and yellow daffodil wallpaper.

Rachel stomped off the snow on a large, fluffy rug before doffing her coat. The doctor carried the garment into the other room. Rachel followed and watched as he spread it on a chair before a low fire burning in the living room hearth. His consideration confused her. She didn't think he liked her much, but he was still polite.

A single lamp had been turned on, sitting on a table beside the flowered sofa. She peered through the shadows, noticing the simple but comfortable recliner, afghan and pillows, family pictures on the mantel, a small television set and a basket of yarn and needles sitting nearby. The surroundings reminded Rachel of Grammy's farm house. Humble but comfortable and inviting. A place where you found refuge from the world.

"Where's Danny?" she whispered.

Placing a finger against his lips, Dr. Thorne beckoned her to follow as he led her down a narrow hall to a bedroom. The door creaked as he pushed it open. The tall shadow of a bunk bed showed her son sleeping soundly in the bottom bed. Another boy about the same age as Danny slept in the top bunk.

Rachel tiptoed across the room and knelt beside her son. She cupped his warm cheek and listened to his even breathing. He gave a deep sigh, his mouth puckering. She could sit and watch him sleep for hours. Knowing he was safe brought her the greatest peace. She could hardly believe complete strangers would take him in, feed him and give him a bed. Dr. Thorne and Gladys's kindness touched her deeply.

A movement beside the door caught her attention. Gladys stood beside her brother wearing a pink bathrobe and fuzzy slippers. Rachel pulled the quilts around Danny's shoulders, then stood and backed out of the room before Gladys closed the door. She followed the doctor into the kitchen where Gladys turned on the light. Rachel blinked her eyes against the sudden brightness.

"How are you feeling?" Gladys asked kindly.

"Better, thank you. I'm sorry for this intrusion. We could go to the motel."

Gladys waved a hand. "Nonsense. They'd charge you sixty-nine dollars for the night. Besides, Sam thinks you have a mild concussion. You'll need someone to look after you and we can't do that over at the motel. Not in this snowstorm."

In the living room, the woman picked up a fresh cotton sheet and flipped it in the air to open it wide. It floated down across the sofa as she made up the Hide-A-Bed.

"Are you hungry?" Gladys asked.

Rachel shook her head, her stomach still queasy.

"Don't worry. You'll feel better tomorrow. Sam tells me you're Myra's granddaughter and you'll be staying out at the Duarte place."

"Yes."

"I knew Myra well. She told me you lived back east."

"Yes, my husband and I lived in Rochester."

Dr. Thorne frowned and shifted his feet, but he didn't say a word. Feeling the weight of his curious gaze, she looked away.

"Let's get you into bed." Gladys flipped off all the lights except the night lamp sitting on a small table beside the Hide-A-Bed.

Now that she'd seen her son, Rachel longed to curl beneath the warm blankets and sleep for a trillion years. In sleep, she could forget her aching heart and the financial troubles plaguing her since Alex died. Even though he'd been gone almost a year, it still felt like she'd lost him just yesterday. She wondered if her heart would ever recover.

"I'll say good-night." Dr. Thorne reached for the door.

"Where are you going in this storm?" Rachel asked before she could stop herself. It wasn't her business.

"When I stay in town, it's usually because we've got a sick animal at the clinic. I'll sleep over there. Gladys will check on you periodically through the night, just to make sure you're okay. She knows what to do."

"Thanks again."

"No problem. I'll see you in the morning." With a nod, he turned and left, a burst of wintry wind echoing his passage.

Rachel stared after him, longing to call him back. She couldn't explain it, but his quiet strength brought her a sense of security. He reminded her just how lonely and vulnerable she'd become over the past year.

"Come on, honey." Gladys led Rachel down the hall, where she dug out a flannel nightgown from a chest of drawers. She retrieved a fluffy bathrobe and a new toothbrush, then showed Rachel to the bathroom.

Ten minutes later, Rachel slid between the chilly covers of her bed and lay awake, too tired to sleep. For just a moment, she allowed herself to feel self-pity. She'd lost her car and couldn't afford another one, her arm was injured, and who knew what shape her possessions inside the travel trailer were in? How was she going to find transportation out to the farmhouse? She couldn't work if she had no wheels to get into town. If only Alex were here. He'd know what to do.

Her situation seemed hopeless, and hot tears wet her cheeks. Then, she remembered God had been with them tonight, guiding and protecting them. It hadn't been easy, but the Lord had brought them through. They could recover, if she just kept her faith.

In the morning, she'd buy a few groceries and find a way out to Grammy's place. Maybe she could hitch a ride with the snowplow. She'd build a new life for herself and Danny. They'd be alone, but they'd be happy and safe.

Sam shivered as he tromped through the snow in his knee-high boots. The storm had tapered off to a light flurry. Nine inches of pristine snow made the night air seem almost as bright as midday. Long shards of ice crystals hung from bare tree branches. The only sound was the crunch of his footsteps. Mother Nature's beauty never ceased to astonish him.

Lovely and treacherous, just like a woman.

This small town was no place for a beautiful young woman like Rachel Walker. She could find a better future in a city somewhere.

Sam snorted. She denied receiving any money from her grandmother's estate, but he found that hard to believe. He couldn't help wondering how Rachel had gone through so much money so fast.

He tried to shake off his uncertainty as he kicked the snow off his boots and stepped into the reception area of his clinic. Even though she was a stranger, he couldn't explain his desire to help Rachel. He should keep some distance from her and her son. Yet, their desperation pulled at his heartstrings. The last thing he needed was another shallow, beautiful woman messing up his calm, solitary life. Loving Melanie had brought him enough pain. And in the end, he'd destroyed whatever happiness they might have shared.

Rachel had no car, very few possessions, and a small son to support. When Sheriff Lloyd looked through her purse for some ID, he'd found her billfold. It consisted of exactly one thousand six hundred and two dollars and eighty-nine cents. No cell phone. No credit cards. No checkbook. Her funds wouldn't buy her a decent car or groceries for very long.

The Duarte place seemed pretty run-down since Frank died some years ago. The possible repairs needed to the pipes and wiring could take every cent Rachel had in her purse.

And how would she get back and forth between her house and town without a car? In this frigid weather, she and the boy couldn't walk. She'd be all alone out there without a phone or anyone to help with heavy projects. She wasn't strong, he could see that from the size of her shapely arms. And those scars! Although old, he recognized a dog bite when he saw one. Rachel had been attacked, probably using her arms to shield her face until help arrived. Sam could only imagine the internal scars such an experience like that would leave on her mentally. He'd seen her reaction to the animals in his clinic. She didn't say so, but he sensed she had a phobia for canines.

Shaking his head, he walked to the back room and stared at the uncomfortable cot. After he shed his coat, hat and boots, he sat down and reached for the alarm clock sitting close by. He set it for six a.m., one hour away, then wriggled his toes. One poked through a hole in his woolen sock. He'd mend it later, when he finally washed his piles of laundry.

Even Gladys finally stopped telling him he should get a wife of his own. He'd dated quite a bit during veterinarian school, but after Melanie, his heart never took flight again. His career became more important.

Until now.

"Ah, you fool," he castigated himself.

He'd just met Rachel Walker. She needed help. That was why he couldn't get her off his mind. Kind of like feeding and becoming attached to a stray cat. It had nothing to do with her clear blue eyes filled with worry for her son, or the way she'd cried while she was unconscious. From the few things she'd mumbled, he knew her husband's name was Alex and she still mourned the man's death. But he couldn't get involved. Her problems weren't his business.

As he lay back on the cot, he folded his arms behind his head and stared at the ceiling. His nose crinkled, catching Rachel's clean, floral scent.

It felt good to be needed by Gladys and Charlie. There wasn't anything he wouldn't do to keep them safe. He'd accepted his fate as a confirmed bachelor, but he never liked it. He'd been born a family man and never accepted the empty hole in his heart. Except for Gladys and Charlie, he'd been alone most of his life. Even God had abandoned him after he lost Melanie.

For some reason, Rachel Walker dredged this up in his mind. The longing. The regrets.

He yearned for someone to shower his love upon. Someone all his own who loved him in return. No matter how full his life got, he'd never get used to the emptiness in his heart.

Or the loneliness.

Chapter Three

Rachel awoke to the smell of bacon frying. She opened her eyes, blinking at the bright sunlight filtering through the lacey curtains in Gladys's living room. The snow had stopped.

Turning her head, Rachel saw Danny and another boy she assumed was Charlie sitting together in the recliner next to the Hide-A-Bed. The boys giggled, their legs dangling over the seat as they stared at her.

"See? I told you she'd wake up soon," Danny told the other boy.

She smiled, unable to resist the merry twinkle in Charlie's eyes. "Good morning, boys. How are you?"

"Fine," Danny responded.

"You slept in." Charlie's freckled nose crinkled.

Rachel stretched, finding her body stiff and sore from the accident. Thinking about her crumpled car made her groan. "What time is it?"

Charlie shrugged, raking his short fingers through the unruly mop of red hair falling over his brow. "I don't know."

Danny glanced at the cartoon character watch Alex gave him for his sixth birthday. "Almost eleven o'clock."

Wow! She had slept in, but they'd gone to bed so late.

"Good morning! Are you hungry?" Gladys called from the doorway of the kitchen. She wore her long chestnut hair curled and loose around her shoulders. Dressed in a red checkered apron, she clutched a plastic spatula in one hand.

Rachel sat up and slid her bare feet to the hardwood floor. Still dressed in the nightgown and bathrobe Gladys gave her the night before, she barely felt the cold in the snug house. "I *am* hungry, actually."

"I laid out clean towels in the bathroom. Sam brought your bags in before he left." Gladys pointed the spatula to where Rachel and Danny's blue suitcases sat near the Hide-A-Bed.

"Where did he go?"

"He drove out to his place early this morning, to feed and water his livestock."

"He was able to drive through the snow to Finnegan's Valley?"

Maybe he'd give her and Danny a ride out to Grammy's place. She hated to impose, but she had few options.

"Sure! A country doctor knows how to get around any impediment. His truck has 4-wheel drive with a plow blade attached to the front fender. If he gets stuck, there's a snowmobile and an extra can of gasoline in the back."

Hmm, impressive. Rachel stood and hugged Danny, breathing in his warm, sweet skin. She gave silent thanks they were safe. When she thought of what could have happened last night, she almost shuddered.

She didn't recognize Danny's pajamas and thought he must have borrowed them from Charlie. Both boys wore animal slippers, Charlie's brown with floppy-eared dogs on the insteps, Danny's yellow with ducks that squeaked when he walked. She reached to tickle the boys' ribs with her good hand. Both of them squealed and scrambled away.

Charlie raced to the television set and flipped it on. "Hooray! Now your mom's awake, we can watch cartoons."

Both boys plopped down on a love seat and shared a red afghan for warmth. Charlie worked the remote control, flipping through channels.

Rachel watched her son, who seemed to accept their predicament quite well. In spite of the accident, it lightened her heart to see him so happy.

"While I finish making breakfast, why don't you get ready? Sam should be back any time now," Gladys told Rachel.

This information prompted Rachel into action. Running a hand over the blue bathrobe, she realized she didn't want Dr. Thorne to see her like this. Why she cared about a stranger's opinion, she refused to contemplate. Instead, she hurried to get ready.

Forty minutes later, she emerged from the steaming bathroom dressed in practical blue jeans and a warm sweater, her hair curled and her makeup in place. As she walked into the living room, she saw the Hide-A-Bed had been put away and Gladys had folded the quilts Rachel used the night before. Danny and Charlie now sat at the kitchen table wolfing down pancakes and eggs.

"I know it's several days away, but why don't you and Danny share Sunday dinner with us?" Gladys said.

"Oh, we couldn't impose."

"Nonsense. You'll need time to get settled. I always fix Sunday dinner over at Sam's place. He has a huge kitchen." Gladys stowed the pile of sheets and blankets in a hall closet.

Rachel hesitated. She didn't feel up to cooking much right now. But she wasn't certain what she thought of having dinner at the doctor's home.

"Stop worrying." Gladys squeezed Rachel's good arm.

"You can invite us over to your house later. Now, come have something to eat. You must be starved."

Rachel followed Gladys into the cozy kitchen. She sat at the table, feeling lazy and confused by Gladys's generosity.

"We've already blessed the food, so dig in," Gladys said.

"Sam says our car got totaled in the crash." Danny spoke with both cheeks bulging.

"Don't talk with your mouth full, son." Rachel wished he hadn't reminded her of their ruined car.

"Yes, I saw it. What'll you do for transportation?" Gladys stood at the stove, stirring scrambled eggs.

Rachel looked down at her plate, noticing the small blue corn flowers swirling around the outer edge. The Lord would provide for them. She had to trust in Him. "I'm not sure."

"How are you fixed for money?"

Wow! Gladys was certainly blunt.

"We'll get by."

"We're looking for a receptionist over at the clinic. Do you need a job?" Gladys sat down with her own plate of food.

"I, uh, yes I do."

But at a veterinarian clinic? She squeezed her left forearm, touching the scars beneath the fabric of her sweater. She swallowed, hating to admit dogs scared her to death. Ever since she was eleven years old and a dog belonging to a neighbor had attacked her. She figured goldfish were harmless enough.

"Can you type?" Gladys asked.

"Absolutely!" No more than forty words per minute, but she'd taken some evening classes at the community college in Rochester. She wasn't fast, but she knew word processing and spreadsheet programs. How hard could it be?

"Sam wants someone with lots of receptionist skills. The

last gal he hired couldn't even type. If you want the job, I'd have to get his approval, first."

"That'd be great." If only he agreed. A laugh of relief bubbled up in Rachel's throat. She *might* have a job. Working in a vet clinic wasn't what she had in mind, but her options were pretty slim.

Gladys didn't look at her as she took a bite of syrupy pancake. Rachel got the impression the other woman tried not to smile. "I'll warn you, it's a busy office."

"Sam mentioned you work there, too."

"Yep." Gladys nodded. "We were both raised on a ranch. After my husband died, I brought Charlie to Finley and Sam put me back on my feet. He gave me a fresh start."

"My husband died last year and I miss him terribly."

"Oh, you're a widow, too. I'm sorry." Gladys's eyes crinkled. "No wonder we've become fast friends. We have a lot in common."

Tears burned Rachel's eyes and she looked away. Her sudden emotions ambushed her. The pain of losing Alex still felt raw. Yet the kindness and generosity of these strangers gave her hope that she and Danny could make it here on their own.

A thud sounded outside on the back porch. The kitchen door opened and Sam came inside with a burst of chilly air.

The moment he entered the room, Rachel felt his presence like a tangible thing. She couldn't understand why the doctor would have such an effect on her.

"Brrr! Close that door." Gladys reached to help him off with his heavy coat.

Sam closed the door before removing the beatup cowboy hat from his head. His short, dark hair curled against the nape of his neck. He set his damp gloves on the washing machine, his cheeks and nose red. He smiled, his gaze sliding over to Rachel. "It sure is pretty outside. You boys want to play in the snow?"

"Yeah!" Danny and Charlie answered in unison.

Sam chuckled. "Then you better get dressed."

Charlie hopped off his chair and raced toward his bedroom followed by Danny. Rachel heard the slamming of a door. Whoops of glee and copious amounts of laughter filtered down the hall.

"You'd think it was Christmas morning." Gladys chuckled as she handed Sam a plate of food.

He turned and paused. Rachel felt the weight of his gaze as he stared at her bare toes. Standing, she helped Gladys fill the sink with sudsy water. Sam sat and reached for the butter. "The snow's deep, but we should be able to get out to your place this morning."

Rachel paused as she dried a glass with a dish towel. "I'd really appreciate a ride."

"Sam lives up the road from your place," Gladys chimed in. "He can make sure your furnace is working."

"Yeah, I'll check things out." Sam's voice held no enthusiasm.

"You'll need groceries, too. I packed some canned goods, but you'll need to stop at Granger's to pick up some milk and perishables." Gladys jutted her chin in the direction of a large box sitting by the back door.

"You didn't need to do that." Rachel almost breathed an audible sigh of relief. She had a ride out to Grammy's place.

"It's no trouble."

It'd been six weeks since Grammy lived in the house. Any number of things could have gone wrong. The power could have been knocked out or the old furnace might no longer work. Having Sam and Gladys accompany her out to the house brought her a measure of comfort.

When she glanced at Sam, Rachel couldn't deny the surly

set of his shoulders, nor the way he avoided meeting her eyes. Last night, he'd been kind, even gentle with her. Now, he seemed irritated. She couldn't blame him. He probably had lots to do and resented a woman and kid taking up his valuable time.

"Have you got fuel for the furnace?" Sam asked.

"I don't know." Rachel hadn't thought about that.

"I'll check your propane tank. If not, I'll call Shorty Keller and see when he can get his truck out there to fill the tank."

"I can help you clean the house," Gladys offered. "Sam's a whiz with repairs. There's nothing he can't do. Isn't that right, Sam?"

He mumbled an affirmative answer before taking another bite of food. His cheek bulged as he chewed, and Rachel took his silence as a good sign. There was no mistaking Gladys's confidence in her brother's abilities, but she felt uncomfortable asking for his help. Alex had difficulty installing child locks on the cupboards. He just hadn't been good at fix-it jobs. "I can't tell you how grateful I am."

Gladys lifted her hand and waved the air. "Many hands make light work. It'll be our pleasure to help."

"Um, maybe I should get ready." Rachel was as ready as she'd ever be, but she needed an excuse to get out of this kitchen before she burst into tears of gratitude. She cut through the living room and hurried into the bathroom, where she sat on the edge of the tub for at least five minutes before finally brushing her teeth.

Outside the window, she heard childish laughter in the front yard. She peeked past the flowered curtains and saw Danny and Charlie, both dressed in winter coats, scarves, hats, gloves and boots as they rolled snowballs to make a snowman. No doubt Danny had borrowed some of the clothing from Charlie. Her son's smile melted her heart. She hadn't seen him laugh like this since—

She sighed. They both missed Alex, and she was glad Danny had found a friend like Charlie. Exiting the bathroom, Rachel came up short in the living room when she heard Sam's deep, disapproving voice. The exasperation in his tone was obvious. After listening for a few moments, Rachel realized she now had a bigger problem on her hands.

"I can't believe you want to hire her as our receptionist." Sam shifted his weight on the linoleum floor in the kitchen.

Gladys stood in front of the refrigerator, putting away the milk. Sam waited until she turned and looked at him, but he didn't like the expression on her face. He knew that look. Her stubborn I'm-your-older-and-wiser-sister look.

"You put me in charge of hiring a new receptionist and I want to hire Rachel," Gladys insisted. "She doesn't have much experience, but she'll do better than Tiffany."

He almost groaned. Did she have to bring up Tiffany? The girl had been down on her luck, just like Rachel. Two months after he hired her, the girl absconded with all the money in his safe. Now he had a bad feeling about Rachel. Like knowing you were about to get hit in the jaw, but your hands were tied behind your back so you couldn't protect yourself. "What are Rachel's skills? Can she even type?"

Tiffany had used the hunt-and-peck method, typing with her two index fingers. Sam's busy office needed a receptionist who could take charge and help out.

"Of course," Gladys said. "And she knows word processing and spreadsheet programs. If I can learn, so can she."

"What are her references?"

"Frank and Myra Duarte, two of the finest people I ever knew," Gladys insisted. "I've always been a good judge of character, and that gal will do just fine for us."

He took a deep breath, wondering if he'd ever find a way to tell his sister no. The fact was, he loved Gladys very much, but this was pushing him near the edge. Something about Rachel Walker tore at the deepest recesses of his heart. He'd noticed her pink-painted toenails, so feminine and attractive they made him crazy. He couldn't explain it and didn't want to try. If she were working in his office every day, always underfoot, always smelling like springtime, he sensed he'd have an internal fight on his hands before long. And he'd promised himself he'd never care for another woman again. His heart couldn't take it.

He rolled his shoulders, trying to ease the tension there. "I don't feel good about this, Glad."

"What have you got against her?" Gladys brushed past him and reached for the laundry basket. He stared after her in a daze, watching dumbly as she folded towels and piled them neatly on the clean kitchen table.

"For one thing, she's a complete stranger," he offered lamely.

Gladys spoke without looking up, her fingers working nimbly as she matched pairs of socks. "She comes from good people, Samuel Nathan."

Samuel Nathan. The name Gladys called him when she disapproved of something he'd said or done.

"But we don't know anything about her," he argued. "Her work ethic, her reliability, her integrity."

"She needs a job. She needs our help. Do you want to just throw her out on the street?"

"Of course not, but I don't want to take in strays and give her a job just because you feel sorry for her."

Gladys pursed her lips. "She's sweet as can be. Don't you think it's time you got over Melanie? That was years ago. You need to move on with your life."

"This has nothing to do with Melanie." A swell of anger

washed over him. Even as he said the words, he knew it was a lie. His voice sounded strained as he spoke through gritted teeth.

"Oh, doesn't it? You haven't looked at another woman since. Not until last night."

He snorted. "Stop matchmaking. I'm too old for Rachel."

"Oh, pooh! She's a widow and six years age difference between you doesn't matter much."

"Closer to nine," he snarled. "Did she tell you she's a widow?"

"Yep, and from the look in her eyes, she loved the man."

Well. He felt sorry for her, then. He knew the pain of losing someone he loved and it never left his heart for one single minute. "She's not working for us. Period."

"Now, Sam—"

"I said no." His soft words resonated through the kitchen like a shout. He rarely put his foot down with Gladys, but when he did, he meant it.

Gladys clamped her mouth shut, her lips pursed with disapproval. In her eyes, he saw disappointment and hurt, but he wouldn't budge on this decision. He couldn't take the chance.

Brooding silence followed.

The rattling of the bathroom door announced Rachel's presence before she stepped into the kitchen. Sam stood at the door wearing his coat, hat and gloves. He held the doorknob in a choking grip, desperate to escape. He couldn't help feeling as though he'd just ruined something beautiful. Like a delicate flower crushed beneath the heels of his work boots.

Rachel met his gaze with a challenging lift of her chin, and he hoped she hadn't heard his conversation with Gladys. He felt ashamed for his lack of charity toward this woman. No doubt God would be disappointed in him again. But it was just one more notch on his conscience. Surely God couldn't be any more disappointed in him than He already was. And yet, Sam couldn't look away from Rachel. Something in her eyes held him captive. A sense of quiet strength he didn't fully understand. She was vulnerable, he knew that. Even frightened. Yet, he could see in her eyes that she would do what had to be done, no matter what. For that reason alone, his respect for her grew.

"Ready to go?" she asked.

He exchanged a glance with Gladys. "Yeah."

So much for not getting involved. He turned away, confused to his bones. One minute, he found himself attracted to this woman in ways he couldn't explain. The next minute, he wanted to strangle her and she hadn't done a single thing to him…except walk into his life and make him start to feel again. Old emotions he thought he'd suffocated twelve years earlier. He must set some boundaries.

"I'll be waiting outside." Sam picked up the box of groceries and juggled it as he pushed the screen door wide with his shoulder. It slapped closed behind him as he stepped out onto the back porch. Gladys closed the kitchen door, shutting out the frigid air.

Shutting out him.

Chapter Four

Rachel took a deep breath as she pulled on her coat and followed Sam outside onto the back porch of Gladys's house. Strays! She tensed when she thought of the conversation she'd overheard between the doctor and his sister. She was tempted to tell Dr. Thorne what he could do with his precious receptionist job.

Obviously Sam had been dumped by a woman named Melanie and hadn't gotten over her yet. Now, he seemed to hold a grudge against Rachel.

She wrapped her scarf around her neck and jerked on the thick leather gloves Gladys had loaned her.

She didn't want anyone's help. But she would need it if she was going to make it here in Finley. The thought of accepting anything from Sam Thorne almost frosted her garters, as Grammy was fond of saying.

Thinking of her grandmother and the funny adages she used brought a smile to Rachel's face. And that was when she saw her small travel trailer. Someone had parked it beside the garage. Probably Sam, who currently stood over the front hitch, hooking it to his truck.

She gravitated toward the back, her gaze searching for damage. As she rounded the corner, she gave a sharp exhale. One side of the trailer had been bashed in, no doubt struck by the oncoming truck she had hit last night. She groaned, wondering how severe the damage might be inside. Every possession she owned was inside this trailer.

She joined Sam, wishing she didn't need to speak to him. Her pride still stung from being called a stray. As she drew deep drafts of cold air into her lungs, her nerves settled. "Will it make it out to Grammy's place okay?"

"Sure, the tires are sound," he said without looking up.

She lifted the latch and opened the double doors, peering through the shadowed interior. Tears filled her eyes. Clothing, towels and bedding lay folded in haphazard fashion. The books she'd packed so carefully were now bundled in disorderly piles, their ruined boxes tossed to one side. Her precious photo albums lay heaped together, their torn pages and pictures sitting on top. The rocking chair Alex had given her the day she came home from the hospital with Danny had been moved to one side. The spokes and one bottom rocker lay broken on the blue padded seat. Someone had leaned the chair against the far wall of the trailer so it wouldn't fall over.

Rachel's heart wrenched. She couldn't contain a small moan as she picked up the splintered pieces of wood. Hot tears ran down her cheeks as she caressed the shining oak with her gloved hands. It was just a chair, and yet it meant so much more. Seeing it ruined like this reminded her of Alex's death and her shattered life. How could she ever repair the damage? When would her heart stop aching for her loss? She was too young to be a widow, and Danny was too young to be without his father. Alex should be here, protecting them, loving them—

The crunch of footsteps warned her of someone's presence. She set the broken rocker pieces aside.

"Everything okay?"

Sam! Why did it have to be him witnessing her moment of weakness? Of all the emotions she felt right now, why did he have to see her cry?

Her knees wobbled so hard she feared they might buckle. She took a shuddering breath and turned away. "Yeah, everything's fine."

A handkerchief appeared in front of her nose. Not a tissue, but a genuine, crisply starched, white linen handkerchief with his initials embroidered in one corner. Murmuring her thanks, she accepted his offering and wiped her eyes.

He peered into the trailer. "I tried to tidy up a bit, but I wasn't sure where everything belonged. At least it's out of the weather."

Her throat tightened and a sick feeling settled in the pit of her stomach. He'd sorted through her things! He'd looked through her pictures and folded her quilts and towels and placed her broken rocking chair against the wall.

"Yes, that's fine." She kept her face averted. No doubt her eyes were red and puffy.

"I'm sorry." He laid a hand on her arm.

No, no! She pulled away, unable to accept his compassion. "Do you think you can close the doors for me?"

"Sure. I've got it hitched to my truck so we can take it out to your place."

She stepped back and gave him room to secure the trailer. With his back to her, she dabbed at her eyes, hoping her mascara hadn't smeared all over her face. She watched as he hesitated, standing in front of the rocking chair. When he rested his hands on the splintered wood, she gave a shuddering breath. Somehow, it felt as though he held her heart in his hands. The gesture seemed too personal, too intimate for her to comprehend.

Without another word, he stepped back and closed the trailer doors. Then he turned to face her. In his eyes, she saw compassion and the one thing she just could not accept from this man.

Pity.

She turned away, praying he held his silence. If he said another word, her broken heart would melt and she'd blubber and cry in front of him. And she couldn't get that close to another man. Her heart wasn't ready to let go of Alex yet.

"Rachel, I can take care of the chair for you."

She nodded, realizing it was for the best. No sense in keeping a broken rocking chair just for the memories. He'd toss it into the garbage pile and she'd try to forget about it.

A snowball came out of nowhere and struck Sam firmly on the side of the head. The missile knocked the scruffy cowboy hat off his head, saving Rachel from an embarrassing moment.

They both whirled and stared in surprise. A giggle came from behind Sam's truck and two little heads covered with ski masks popped up. Rachel found herself suddenly bombarded with snowballs.

"Why, you little monsters." Sam laughed, then grabbed Rachel's arm and pulled her with him as he ran for cover. He crouched behind the trailer, scooping up a handful of snow to pack together.

"We're about to get pelted. Look out!" he yelled at Rachel.

She ducked just in time. A snowball exploded against the side of the trailer, inches away from where her head had been. As she stooped beside Sam, more snowballs showered overhead, thudding against the side of the garage or landing harmlessly at her feet.

Sam reached for handfuls of snow, pounding them together in his big, gloved hands. "Don't just sit there, lady. We need ammunition."

His booming voice shook with amusement and she

stared, stunned by this sudden change in him. This couldn't be the same rude man who told her she couldn't work for him. The same man who offered his handkerchief and apology for her loss.

His words spurred her into action and she started making snowballs. Sam fired missiles as fast as Rachel produced them. Soon, Sam gave up on the snowballs and charged. The enemy scattered in a melee of fleeing boots and gleeful screams. Not quite knowing what she should do, Rachel chased after Sam, her ears ringing with laughter.

Sam tackled the boys, rolling with them, flinging snow in their faces. They clung to the big man like two small koala bears.

"No fair, Sam," Danny yelled. "You're bigger than us."

Rachel laughed, until her sides ached and tears ran from her eyes. And when she realized what was happening, it made her heart stand still and she felt such poignancy that she gasped with pain.

Alex never played with her and Danny like this. He'd been romantic in his own way, but never spontaneous. He'd played with her and Danny, but in a dignified, remote sort of way, usually from a park bench or with a board game between them. In the six years they'd been married, she'd only heard Alex belly-laugh twice. Never this up-close-and-personal, undignified heap rolling at her feet.

"Okay, okay, I give!" Sam held up his arms and stood before dusting snow off his coat and blue jeans.

When Danny threw his arms around Sam's long legs in a bear hug, Rachel's mouth dropped open, and she stared wide-eyed. "Let's do it again, Sam. Let's do it again!" Danny cried.

Over the tops of the boys' heads, Sam met Rachel's eyes. His face flushed a deep red. Then he looked away, breaking the magical moment. No doubt he'd remembered who she was and how she came to be here and that was that.

"Ahem." Sam cleared his voice, and he stepped away from Danny. "I think we'd better get going. Daylight's a'burning."

"Yay! Let's go to your place," Charlie hollered as he ran toward Sam's truck.

Danny followed. Both boys yelled excitedly.

Gladys came out of the house carrying a picnic basket. Sam took the basket and placed it in back, then helped her into the truck before reaching to take Rachel's elbow.

"Careful, it's slick." He leaned his head down, his words brushing against her cheek. His nearness made her feel giddy.

As she stepped up on the high foot rail and climbed inside, she heard the window defroster running against the windshield. Sam got into the driver's seat. Even with Gladys sitting between them, his attention unnerved Rachel.

He shifted the truck into gear, ready to pull out of the driveway, but then looked in the rearview mirror. "Buckle up, boys. We've got a bumpy ride ahead of us."

The drive out to Grammy's place didn't take long. When they hit the dirt road, Sam shifted his truck into 4-wheel drive and skimmed through the drifts of snow with steady ease.

Rachel pointed off to the distance. "Danny, there's our house."

Danny scooted forward against the backseat, leaning his face over her shoulder to get a better view out the window. She reached back her hand and pressed her palm against his face.

The old 1930s farmhouse and barn sat together in a field of white, a single power line leading out to the house. Painted white, the clapboard boasted nothing special except a quaint charm left dowdy by years of neglect. Fruit trees surrounded the front yard with limbs void of leaves and covered with frost and icicles. Snowladen evergreens edged the long gravel driveway. The top of the fence line stood just visible above the blanket of snow.

A classic winter scene.

"There's Uncle Sam's place," Charlie shot a finger toward a large, modern house about a quarter of a mile down the road.

Slim colonnades lined the wraparound porch, supporting a pretty portico and balcony on the second story. The porch framed the first floor. The white clapboard and blue trim looked newly painted. A detached four-car garage painted the same color as the house sat nearby, along with spacious corrals.

An enormous, shiny-roofed barn nestled in the small valley beside the pond brought Rachel awe. When she came here to visit Grammy just before Alex died, the house hadn't been finished and Sam didn't live here yet. This was where he planned to build his large animal hospital. Impressive, considering he'd built his home on land that used to belong to her grandparents. Rachel remembered a time when herds of grazing cattle and horses roamed these fields. She couldn't begrudge Sam. It seemed fitting that he make use of the land he'd purchased from her grandmother.

"Hey, Mom, we have a lake," Danny exclaimed.

She looked at the body of water nestled in the valley between her farmhouse and Sam's place. A thin layer of ice had formed over its surface, the shore edged with tufts of frozen sedge grass, cattails, and tall elm trees. The tops of posts jutting above the snow showed where the small dock sat on the east side, close to Grammy's farmhouse.

"That's not a lake," Charlie laughed. "It's a pond. In the summertime, ducks and geese nest along the shore. You should see the baby goslings. They're so cute."

Rachel pointed at the dock, where a tall tree stood out over the water. A thin rope with a big, black tire hung from one sturdy branch. "I used to sit on the dock with a fishing line. Some of my happiest memories are of swinging on that tire before plunging into the water below. Grandpa always swam with me while Grammy laid out a picnic lunch for us to enjoy."

"You think we can fish there again?" Danny pressed his nose against the window.

"I'm not sure. Grandpa seeded plump rainbow trout into the pond for that very purpose, but the fish might be all gone, now."

"Can we go ice skating?" Danny asked.

"No!" The adults responded simultaneously.

Sam looked in the rearview mirror. "You mustn't ever go out on that ice, Danny. It's not safe. You'd fall through. Okay?"

Danny shot him a mutinous frown. "Okay."

Sam flashed Rachel a grin over the top of Gladys's head and she couldn't resist smiling back. At times, being with him felt so comfortable and normal. Like she and Danny actually belonged here.

What a crazy notion.

A distant look flashed in Sam's eyes and he frowned, as if an unpleasant memory had surfaced. He looked away, his jaw tight.

"I hope we're not keeping you from something important," Rachel said.

"Of course not. Don't be silly," Gladys responded.

Sam looked straight ahead. Rachel peered out the back window, checking the progress of her travel trailer as it sloshed through the slush.

As they pulled into the yard at Grammy's place, a large black Labrador came out of nowhere, barking. Sam parked the vehicle, and the noisy animal bounded toward Rachel's side of the truck, jumping up to plant its front paws on the window. Rachel scooted back, gaping in horror at rows of sharp teeth and a damp, black nose. Even with the glass and metal of the door shielding her, memories of terror and pain swamped her. The dog barked over and over again. Rachel's body ached with fear and a rush of panic caused her pulse to hammer in her ears. She felt as though her lungs might explode and dug her fingernails into the cloth seat.

Oh, please! Don't let me faint now.

"Go away!" her voice squeaked.

Sam opened his door and slid out of the truck. "It's okay, Rachel. It's my dog and I'll take care of him. Wait here for a few minutes."

That suited Rachel fine.

Sam clapped his hands, calling to the big dog. "Shadow! Come here, you mangy mongrel. Don't you have any manners?"

Gladys patted Rachel's knee. "I don't know why Shadow's over here at your place. He should be home minding his business."

The dog bounded over and jumped up on Sam, growling playfully as the man rubbed the animal's ears. From the backseat, Danny rested his hand on Rachel's shoulder, his blue eyes creased with worry. "It's okay, Mommy. Sam won't let his dog hurt you."

Her son's concern touched her heart. She didn't fully understand her own phobia. She tried to tell herself everything was okay, yet she couldn't seem to gain control over her anxiety.

Sam pushed the dog away and pointed toward his place. "Go home, Shadow. Go!"

The dog whined, then took off like a shot and Rachel breathed a sigh of relief.

"There, everything's fine now." Gladys smiled.

Sam came and opened Rachel's door slow and careful. "You okay, now?"

Her voice came out as a small, indistinguishable croak. Instead, she nodded, wishing he hadn't seen visible proof of her fear.

"Shadow won't bother you again. Come on." He reached

to take her hand and guide her out of the truck. The little boys followed, scrambling into the yard.

Rachel looked at the house. Peeling paint covered the white clapboard. The green trim appeared dull and faded. A shutter hung loose at an odd angle against the outside wall. Half of the picket fence had fallen over, buried in the depths of snow. The front windows stared back at them, black and vacant.

Just like her heart.

She waited beside Gladys while Sam used the plow blade on his front fender to clear the driveway. When he finished, he called to the boys who romped in the snow. "Let's see if we can clear a path to the front door. I've got plenty of snow shovels, so I'll expect you boys to help. Let's get this place cleaned up."

Sam's take-charge manner gave Rachel confidence. As the boys scrambled to help, Sam lifted three snow shovels out of the back. He handed one to each child. Rachel pulled on her gloves. "How can I help?"

"I'm out of shovels. You and Gladys can supervise and let your injured arm heal. Once we clear a path to the house, you can go inside."

Rachel stood in the deep snow, her feet warm and snug in the boots Gladys had loaned her. The women waited as the boys and Sam bent their backs to the work. Sam shoveled snow away from the picket fence. His heavy thigh muscles flexed beneath his blue jeans as he cleared a wide path, revealing gravel and then the cement walkway leading up to the front porch. As he worked, his breath came out in little puffs. His lean cheeks reddened and he sniffed against the cold air. Occasionally, he glanced at his progress, then went back to work.

Realizing she was staring, Rachel turned and went to the back of the truck and opened the travel trailer. With Gladys's help, they sorted her things and stacked boxes.

Within an hour, the boys had cleared all the walkways leading up and around the house, barn and tool shed.

Danny wiped his red nose on the back of his coat sleeve. "Are we done yet?"

Sam surveyed their work and nodded. "Yep! Good job, boys. You've earned some free time."

Danny beamed with happiness, looking as proud as if he'd built a skyscraper with a box of toothpicks and a roll of duct tape.

"Hey, come on! Let's check out the barn," Charlie yelled to Danny.

"Be careful," Rachel called. "Don't climb into the loft until we can check it out. No telling what shape the timbers are in."

"Okay," they both said.

The boys hooted with laughter as they ran through the snow, their short legs sinking deep to midthigh as they slogged toward the gray structure.

Rachel went with Sam and Gladys to the front door, feeling suddenly nervous and unsure. No longer did the house look like the comfortable, inviting friend where she spent so many childhood summers with her grandparents. Now it seemed a barren, cold building. Like a stranger, abandoned and unloved. Resentful.

"Careful, it's slippery. I'll check the barn in a few minutes to see if I can find some ice melt." Sam reached out and took each woman by the elbow, guiding them up to the front porch. His touch felt like a bolt of electricity shooting up Rachel's arm, but she couldn't bring herself to pull away to save her life.

Gladys removed her gloves and turned the knob, but the door didn't budge. "Do you have a key?"

As Rachel dug into her purse, she couldn't suppress a feeling of excitement and also a sinking into dread. The last time she was here had been to close up the house after Grammy died.

Finding the key, her hand shook as she tried to insert it into the lock.

"Allow me." Sam's strong fingers folded over hers, the warmth of his hand seeping into her bones. She pulled back as if burned and watched mutely as he inserted the key. The lock gave with a hollow click. He turned the doorknob, but the door resisted. He pushed harder and it gave with a scraping sound.

"Hmm, the wood's probably swelled with this cold weather," he observed. "I have a planer over at my place and can shave the edges so the door fits better."

"Thank you, I'd appreciate it." Rachel's voice sounded vague.

Pushing the portal wide, he stood back, holding the screen door open. "Ladies first."

He gave Rachel a smile of encouragement, and she felt grateful to have him here.

As they stepped inside, Rachel expected the scent of cinnamon and roses…the smell she associated with Grammy. Instead, she caught the odor of a closed-up house. Freezing cold enveloped her as she stared through the dark shadows of the living room. When she'd closed up the house, she'd hired someone from town to drain the water pipes so they wouldn't freeze once they turned off the water. If she had power and heat, she would just need a sturdy broom and mop to clean out the dust. Soon the house would seem like the old friend she once knew. In no time, she and Danny would feel right at home.

Dim sunlight filtered through the draperies in the living room. Except for the cobwebs crisscrossing the corners of the room, everything looked just as she had left it.

Dreary and forlorn.

Chapter Five

Inside the farmhouse, dark shadows hovered about the living room. Sam reached over and clicked on the light, thinking the place looked like it was still in mourning.

Rachel gasped with delight, staring at the old-fashioned fixture hanging from the high ceiling of the living room. Sam liked the way her eyes crinkled when she smiled. Somehow the house didn't seem so sinister anymore.

"That's a good sign," he murmured as he looked about.

Gladys went to inspect the kitchen, leaving him alone with Rachel. She gazed at a white mound sitting in front of the fireplace, then pulled the sheet off and stared at the threadbare recliner.

"Something wrong?" he asked.

"No, I was just remembering happy times when Grandpa would rest back in this easy chair after supper, a glass of fresh-squeezed lemonade in his hand. He read to us from the Scriptures every evening. Grammy always sat beside him on the sofa, her nimble fingers working the knitting needles as she made another colorful afghan, scarf or sweater."

"Yeah," Sam agreed. "I can picture Frank and Myra sitting

in this room just as you've described. I never met two people who loved the Lord more than them."

"I don't mean to be rude, but you don't strike me as the religious type."

He supposed she was right. Since he lost Melanie, he never went to church, prayed, or worshiped the Lord. And yet, he still believed in God. He just hadn't forgiven Him for taking Melanie away. "You might be surprised. After my folks died, Frank Duarte took me to church every week. While we worked out in the fields, he taught me a lot about the Lord. He taught me honesty and integrity, too. Frank was a good man I highly respected."

She smiled, her eyes glazed with tears. "My grandparents took me to church, too, when I came to stay with them in the summer months. Together, they answered my questions about God and who I was and why I'm here. If not for them, I never would have learned about my Father in Heaven, who loves and cares for me. That knowledge was all that sustained me after Alex died."

Her confession left him a bit shaken. He didn't expect her to talk about her dead husband. It seemed a bit too personal and made him feel close to her, something he couldn't allow. He cleared his throat.

"Sam, I need to explain about the dog." She took a deep breath, as if bracing herself.

"Only if you want to." Who was he kidding? He was dying to know the truth. But this was something she'd have to take at her own pace. He sensed he shouldn't push her.

"When I was very young, I was attacked by a huge black dog. I ended up with sixty-two stitches and rabies shots. I've never gotten over it."

So, that explained the scars on her forearms as well as her

unrealistic fear of Shadow. She definitely had a right to be wary of dogs.

She stepped away and the vulnerable look on her face melted his heart. He realized in that moment that he held the power to hurt her. "Most dogs are quite gentle and affectionate. Maybe in time, you'll learn to like them."

She hesitated, her delicate brow knit together with doubt. He caught the subtle movement of her trembling body. A crazy notion flitted across his brain, to take her into his arms and comfort her.

Gladys returned, breaking the uncomfortable silence. "You're lucky we're a small community and your house is far enough outside of town that no kids vandalized the place."

Sam stepped away. "Let's see what we've got to deal with. Where's the thermostat for the furnace?"

"Back there." Rachel pointed at the narrow hallway leading to the bedrooms and the stairway leading to the upper floor. Without a word, Sam headed in that direction, wondering why he felt so out of sorts. He'd make sure Rachel and her son were comfortable and safe, and then he'd forget about them. No big deal.

Or was it?

Rachel remained in the living room, gathering up dust cloths and drawing back the drapes. Sunlight filtered through the dingy windows. She walked about the room, perusing the humble furnishings piece by piece. In spite of the sheets, a layer of dust covered the oak coffee table, side tables, magazine rack and bookshelf. Once she took a dust cloth and can of polish to them, they would gleam beautifully.

She surveyed the carpet and upholstery of the sofa and chairs. When had they become so faded and threadbare? She'd clean them and make do for the time being.

Feeling more optimistic, she walked through the house with Gladys, jotting down notes on a pad of paper. "I have cleaning supplies in my travel trailer. A stiff-bristled broom, dustpan, mop and bucket, cleansers, rags, vacuum cleaner—"

Sam poked his head around the corner, startling them. "I turned on the heat, but nothing happened. I brought a variety of filters with me, and I'll change the old ones and check out the furnace, but I think you're out of propane."

"Call Shorty Keller. He should come out and fill her propane tank today," Gladys ordered.

"I'll tell him this is an emergency." Sam reached into his pants pocket and withdrew his cell phone, flipping it open. Within moments, he had someone on the phone and arranged to have the propane tank filled within the hour.

"I could never get that kind of service in the city. How did you get him to agree to come out so soon?" Rachel asked, as Sam pocketed his phone.

He shrugged and flashed a smile. "I'm his vet. Besides, Shorty and I are good friends. Everyone knows everyone here in Finley. We can't have someone living without heat in this cold weather."

Relief settled over Rachel. She owed a lot to Sam and Gladys.

Sam continued his work on the furnace while Gladys went out to the travel trailer. Rachel walked through the house, opening blinds and curtains, checking the status of doors and windows, beds, dressers and carpets.

In her grandparent's bedroom, she inspected the teeny closet and tripped over a loose floorboard.

"Ooff!" She struck the wall. Rubbing her shoulder, she eyed the rough floors. Grammy had often told her to replace the flooring once she died, but Rachel didn't have that kind of money. Maybe she could get some warm throw rugs to help with the problem. And a hammer and nails.

Rachel helped Gladys bring in the contents of her travel trailer, stacking the boxes along one wall in the living room. She noticed the absence of her rocking chair and figured Sam must have thrown it away.

"If it's okay with you, I think we should divide up the work. I'll tackle the bathroom. It doesn't look too bad." Gladys picked up a bucket, cleanser and cleaning rags.

Rachel agreed. "And I'll get the beds set up so we have a place to sleep."

Sam headed for the back door. "I'll turn on the water, so you have something to clean with."

Moving to the back storage room, Rachel intended to check the condition of the washer and dryer. Glass crunched beneath her feet and she looked down. What on earth—

A chilling breeze swept past her face and she turned. A broken window. The wind caused one barren tree branch of Grammy's apple tree to smack against the outside wall. Startled, Rachel whirled around...and ran straight into Sam's arms.

"Umph!" he grunted, as she thumped against his solid chest.

"Excuse me!" Her nose filled with the spicy scent of his cologne. Embarrassment heated her cheeks as she stepped back and looked up at his face.

"Hey, where's the fire?" He steadied her, his deep voice rumbling in his chest.

"I have a broken window. The wind startled me and I—" She stared up into his eyes, seeing the flecks of gold, the crinkle of kindness at the corners, the slight stubble on his chin.

"Where?"

"There." She pointed without looking in that direction. She blinked, realizing she was staring, and continued to do so for several pounding moments.

She stepped back, feeling an invisible connection to this man, like an electrical current buzzing through the air. She didn't understand the attraction. Not when she was still so in love with Alex.

He glanced at the window. "I've got some sturdy plywood in the back of my truck. I'm sure I can board the window up until we can replace it with glass. We better make a list."

She held up her notepad for his inspection. "I've already started one."

"Good. Add some gaskets for the furnace."

He sounded so domestic and she felt odd inside. Safe and comfortable, yet betrayed by her own feelings.

After Sam tightened all the bolts on the bed frames, Rachel shook out the sheets to make up the beds. Crossing the floor in the room that had been occupied by her grandmother, she again tripped on the loose floorboard, almost doing a header into the closet. She staggered over to the chest of drawers, arching her back, hoping she hadn't pulled any muscles.

"Land sakes alive!" Gladys exclaimed from the living room.

"What's the matter?" Rachel called.

"I think you'd better get in here, honey."

Now what? Rachel raced down the hall, pulling up short when she saw Gladys standing in front of the bookshelf, a rag clutched in one hand, a dusty book in the other. At her feet lay two twenty-dollar bills.

"What—?"

"They fell out of the book when I picked it up to dust it," Gladys explained.

Rachel's eyes widened. She knew Grammy never trusted banks and always paid her bills with cash, but it never occurred to her that she might hide money in her books.

Gladys' eyes sparkled. "Do you think there's more?"

Both she and Rachel reached for the books at the same time. In a matter of fifteen minutes, they pulled every book off the shelves. Holding them upside down by the spine, the women fanned the pages to reveal any more hidden treasures.

Sam found them there, sitting in a pile of money. "What's going on?"

They quickly explained and he chuckled, running his fingers through his short hair. "How much money is here?"

They counted the bills and Sam gave a low whistle. "Four hundred and sixty dollars."

"The good Lord provides in strange ways," Gladys observed.

Rachel wrapped her arm around Gladys's waist for just a moment. "You've got that right. Thank you for finding the money. I can't tell you how grateful I am. Maybe I'll be able to afford a car that actually includes a steering wheel."

The women laughed. Sam studied the room, as if looking for other possible hiding places. "Do you think there's more, or were the books her only stash of cash?"

Rachel shook her head, wondering at her grandmother's eccentricity. "There's no way to know for certain without searching."

Gladys hopped to her feet and they all joined her on a foray around the house.

"Eureka!" Sam called from Danny's bedroom.

They raced to join him, chuckling as they peered over his shoulder. A table lamp lay on Danny's bed, the base revealing a hollow bottom. In Sam's hand, he clutched a one-hundred-dollar bill. Rachel gasped.

Gladys hooted with laughter. "Pay dirt. Who knows how much money that old gal might have hidden around this house?"

They searched for more, but didn't find anything. Still, Rachel couldn't help feeling incredibly blessed. She needed the money, and it would certainly make her and Danny's lives easier.

"Hello! Anyone home?"

"That'll be Shorty." Sam brushed past Rachel and walked to the living room, where the two men greeted each other.

The women followed and Gladys made the introductions.

Shorty mirrored his name, standing not much taller than Rachel. He had stocky legs and wide shoulders, and was dressed in heavy coveralls. He removed the bright orange hunter's cap from his bald head and took her hand.

"Glad to make your acquaintance. I been filling Myra's propane tank for years. Now I know you're here, I'll come out and top your tank off every couple of weeks. Don't want you to run out in this cold." The freckles across his nose crinkled as he smiled wide.

"Thank you." Rachel withdrew her hand from his tight grip.

Shorty looked around the room. "I'm also a good electrician, if you need help in that department."

"There's not much Shorty can't do," Gladys said.

"How about plumbing?" Rachel asked.

"Yep! And roofing, too."

"Can you remove tree stumps? Come spring, I'd like to take a couple of old stumps out of the front yard."

"That, too."

Sam stepped closer to Rachel's side, a territorial movement. Surely she imagined it.

"Is there anything you don't do?" Rachel asked, trying to ignore the butterflies in her stomach.

"Hair and nails," Shorty quipped. "And I don't do windows. I'll replace 'em, but I don't clean 'em."

They laughed, but Rachel noticed Sam's smile seemed forced.

"Why don't I help you fill that propane tank?" Sam urged Shorty toward the front door, leaving Rachel and Gladys inside.

Watching the men go, a feeling of warmth enveloped Rachel. She had friends here and people who went out of their way to make sure she and Danny were safe.

By the time Sam and Gladys left later that afternoon, the house was clean, toasty warm, and Shorty had replaced the broken window. Now, if Rachel could just resolve her transportation problem and find a job.

Chapter Six

The next morning, Sam drove over to Rachel's house in his old junker truck. He couldn't explain why he'd come out here. He seemed to find himself in the truck and driving down the road before he realized what he was doing.

Rachel must have heard him pull up out front. She came outside and stood on the front porch, hugging herself against the biting cold.

As he got out of the clunker, she smiled so bright it made his jaw ache. The morning sun glinted off her golden hair, and he thought her the most beautiful woman he'd ever seen.

"Good morning," she greeted him. "You're driving a different vehicle today."

Vehicle? He glanced at the clunker. He'd pounded the right front fender out after an enraged steer rammed the truck. The blue paint job had long since faded and peeled, replaced by rust and age. "I guess you can call it a vehicle. It doesn't look like much, but it's solid and has a lot of power on these bad roads."

"What brings you out our way?"

He didn't know for sure. He just knew he had to see her

again. "I thought I'd stop by and make sure you're okay. Is the furnace still working okay?"

"Yes, and we've got hot water."

"Good." As he stepped up on the porch, he jerked the scruffy hat off his head. For several moments, he stood mesmerized by the sight of her in faded blue jeans and a thick, red sweater.

"Sam!" Danny yelled, as he burst past the screen door and flung his arms around Sam's legs.

"Hi, pal. How was your first night in the house?"

"Good! But the TV doesn't work too good and we have mice." Danny's nose crinkled with repugnance as he hopped up and down in his Rocketman jammies.

Sam chuckled and ruffled the boy's hair. "I'll check the TV. We don't have cable out here, but an antenna should help. And a few good mousers will take care of that problem."

"Mousers?" Rachel asked, as they went inside.

"Yeah, cats. They're great to have around when you live on a farm."

She looked doubtful, and he remembered her phobia for dogs.

"I figured you'd need a ride into town, to run some errands and buy more supplies."

Her face flushed with embarrassment. "I do, but surely you have better things to do with your time."

True, and yet he couldn't seem to help himself. He just couldn't stay away. She had no transportation into town, and for some crazy reason he felt responsible for her. "It's no trouble, Rachel."

"I appreciate it." She turned to face her son. "You better get dressed, young man. We're going to town."

"Yippee!" the boy yelled, as he raced to his bedroom.

"I better get ready, too." She disappeared down the hall and Sam sat on the sofa, looking about.

Most of the boxes they'd brought in from the travel trailer were gone. Rachel must have stayed up late unpacking. The room looked tidy and comfortable, with afghans, pillows and family pictures set about. He found himself wishing he lived here instead of over at his big, modern, and very lonely house.

"Okay, let's go." Rachel bustled toward the front door with Danny in tow.

Outside, Sam helped them into the clunker. "The sun's bright today. Looks like we're gonna have a good melt-off."

"Oh, I hope so," Rachel said. "We need clear roads. I may have to walk for a while until I find a job and get a new car."

Her needs weighed heavily on Sam's mind, but he didn't know how to broach the subject plaguing him. He didn't want to help this woman and her child, and yet he couldn't seem to stop himself. She needed a job.

They didn't talk as Sam drove into town. On Center Street, he gazed out his window at the houses and shops bathed in pristine snow. "Anyone feel like a cup of hot chocolate from the diner?"

"Yeah!" Danny yelled.

Sam pulled into a parking place in front of Claridge's Diner. Rachel didn't wait for him to open her door as they all clambered out of the truck. She paused beside the front window of the café where a blue sign read: Waitress Wanted.

Oh, no! Sam shouldn't have brought her here.

As they entered the café, a gold bell tinkled over the door. They stepped up to the front counter, and Danny sat on a red cushioned stool with duct tape across the top to keep the yellow stuffing inside.

Rachel glanced at the white walls dimmed by layers of grime. "Nothing's changed much since I was a child, except the place looks rather shabby."

"Yeah, the diner's gone downhill since Mr. Claridge passed away," Sam said in a low voice.

A tall, thin man emerged from the back kitchen wearing a white T-shirt and an apron stained by grease. Stubble on his chin showed he hadn't shaved in several days. His flaccid face gleamed with perspiration. The man's gaze glanced off Danny before landing on Rachel. A lewd smile split his thin lips as he leaned across the counter and looked her up and down.

The minute they entered Claridge's Diner, Sam regretted bringing them here. Dwayne Claridge usually worked the evening shift. Cherise, one of the waitresses who lived out in the valley, probably couldn't make it in to work today because of the bad roads. Sam thought Dwayne must have opened the restaurant that morning.

"What can I get you folks?" Dwayne asked, his voice friendly, his gaze devouring Rachel.

"Three hot chocolates to go." Sam took a protective step closer to Rachel. This used to be a nice family diner before Dwayne drove it into the ground. Sam couldn't explain it, but he wanted Rachel out of this hole in the wall and back inside the warm cab of his truck. Right now.

"Sure!" Dwayne grinned at Rachel as he reached for the foam cups. "You're not from around these parts, are you?"

"Uhm, no," Rachel answered, her voice filled with uncertainty.

"We live at my great-grandma's house," Danny piped in.

"Oh? And who's your grandma, son?" Dwayne filled each cup with hot chocolate from the machine.

"Myra Duarte." The boy's voice rang with pride.

"That so? You're living out at the Duarte place, huh?" Dwayne topped each cup off with a generous shot of whipped cream then placed a clear bubble lid over the top. Sam glanced at Rachel, wanting to say something, but not knowing what.

Dwayne inserted a plastic straw through the openings of the cups. As he placed them on the counter beside the cash register, he smiled suggestively at Rachel. "Be careful, now. They're hot."

She politely ignored his flirting and pointed at the sign in the window. "I noticed your advertisement for a waitress."

Something cold gripped Sam's chest. He should have seen this coming.

Dwayne leaned closer. "That's right. Are you looking for a job, honey?"

"No, she's not. What do I owe you?" Sam whipped out his wallet, not caring in the least that he sounded rude. Though he didn't look at Rachel, he felt her disapproval. He couldn't help himself. He bristled with fury. Since high school, Dwayne had a reputation for making vulgar advances toward women. The thought of Rachel working here and enduring Dwayne's crudity brought a sickening lump to Sam's gut.

Sam glanced at Rachel and found her twisting her leather gloves with her hands. He remembered how she'd stood at the back of her travel trailer, crying over her broken rocking chair and photos of her life with her dead husband. After the accident, he'd studied her picture until he felt as though he knew the couple like good friends. Danny looked just like his father; the same blue eyes, blond hair and pointed nose. Handsome in a pretty sort of way. Not the type of man Sam thought Rachel would choose.

Now, for some crazy reason, Sam felt responsible for her. Like he needed to protect her from creeps like Dwayne Claridge. But she still needed a job to provide for her son. He'd been unfair to resist Gladys's efforts to hire Rachel. The job at the clinic would be perfect for her, but it wouldn't be perfect for him.

"That'll be five thirty-four." The cash register chinged as Dwayne opened the drawer.

"Keep the change." Sam slapped six dollars on the counter and reached for the cups, handing one to Danny.

"Let's go," Sam jerked his head toward the front door of the diner. Danny moved in that direction, but Rachel hesitated.

"Now, about that job. Do you have any work experience?" Dwayne rested his elbows on the counter and Sam resisted the urge to connect his fist with Dwayne's nose.

Rachel's eyes filled with wary desperation, as if she wanted to flee, but she didn't dare pass up an opportunity for employment. "Yes, I worked for several years as a waitress in Rochester."

Sam shifted his booted feet, feeling antsy. Wishing he could get her to leave.

"We could give you a try." A wide grin spread across Claridge's grizzled face.

A leaden weight settled in Sam's chest and he could barely breathe. He felt as though he were drowning. If he didn't do something fast, he'd regret it the rest of his life. And he already had too many regrets to carry another burden.

As he opened his mouth to speak, he felt as though he stood on a precipice, lifting his foot to step off into the deep, dark void above the jagged cliffs far below.

"She's already got a job at my clinic. Now let's go." Sam took her arm and steered her toward the door. Thankfully, she didn't resist.

Rachel stared over her shoulder at Claridge, stuttering in astonishment. "But I thought—"

Claridge stared after them in surprise. Outside by the truck, Rachel jerked her arm free and glared at Sam with wide, angry eyes. "Just what do you think you're doing?"

Danny waited beside the truck, sipping the hot liquid in his cup. At her angry voice, he stopped and looked at her, his expression filled with doubt.

"I heard what you said to your sister about not hiring me," Rachel whispered in a hostile voice. Sam couldn't blame her. He tried to apologize, but a lump formed in his throat. A lock of blond hair fell over her face before she tucked it behind her ear. His fingers itched to touch that silky softness. To take back every surly word he'd said to her. A yearning filled him so intense that he couldn't speak. Couldn't breathe.

Doyle Longley and his daughter waved as they crossed the street. Sam hated to have this conversation with Rachel out in public. "Can we please get in the truck now?"

Rachel rested one hand on her hip. If he weren't feeling so out of sorts over being jealous, he might have smiled at her posture. She looked madder than a caged squirrel and absolutely beautiful, with her blond hair framing her angry face.

She tilted her head to one side, her pretty mouth pressed with disapproval. "You don't want me working for you. So, why would you jeopardize my chance to find another job?"

"Look, I made a mistake," Sam confessed. "I need a receptionist, but I was...I was uncertain because I don't really know anything about you."

But he wanted to.

"And how do you think I feel? What do I really know about *you*?" Rachel fired back.

She had him there. He could think of no response.

"I have a child to support. I need a job and I can't afford to be choosy." She jabbed her finger toward the diner.

"You have a job. You'll work for me at the clinic." He tried to be firm without being too pushy. He sensed Rachel was the kind of woman who wouldn't be forced.

She shook her head, her blue eyes flashing fire. "I'll work for whomever I choose. You can't order me around, Samuel Nathan Thorne."

Yep, he'd hit that nail on the head. He almost smiled at the

way she said his name, just like Gladys did when she was irritated with him. Instead, he lifted his hands to try and calm
her down. And that amazed him most of all. Since when did
he care if a woman got irritated with him?

"I don't mean to order you, Rachel. I just don't want you
to work for Claridge. I'd really like you to work as my receptionist. I pay more and it'll be a better job with benefits. You
won't need child care if you work for me."

Her fingers toyed with the fringe along the edge of her
scarf. "But I thought you didn't want me—"

He couldn't resist the pull forcing him to do everything
short of begging. He wanted to forget the whole thing, and
yet an inner force drove him onward. As if he no longer spoke
for himself. "I've reconsidered. Now, can we please go?"

"I don't understand." The stubborn tilt of her chin told him
he'd have to offer more explanation.

"If you work for Claridge, you'll be ogled and proposi-
tioned every day. I can't let that happen."

Her mouth rounded and her face flushed an adorable
shade of pink. She looked down at her son who stood
hugging her side and scowling at Sam. "I...I felt uncomfortable around Mr. Claridge, but I didn't believe he might take
advantage of me—"

"Yeah, he's been that way since high school. I've known
him all my life. No good woman should work for him. You're
just gonna have to trust me on this."

"But I don't want any handouts."

Sam lifted his shoulders in a shrug. "I expect a fair day's
work for a fair day's pay."

Her eyes met his and he felt lost in the color of sea blue.

"I need health insurance and...and a dental plan," she said.

"Fine. We've already got a medical plan set up."

At that moment, Sam would have given her the moon,

stars and world peace if he could. Instead, he cleared his voice, his throat feeling like sandpaper. He'd let down his guard, but no more. She could work for him, but that was it. No more romping around in the yard having snowball fights with her kid, and no more gazing into those beautiful eyes of hers. He had to protect his heart.

Marvin Sewell, the bank manager, came out of the post office and scurried toward the bank without his winter coat. Dressed in a navy blue business suit, Marvin wrapped his arms around himself to ward off the cold. Danny looked up and his eyes widened as he stared after the man's retreating back, but Sam paid little heed to the boy.

"Daddy!" Danny jerked away from Rachel, dropping his cup of hot chocolate to the ground. The liquid splattered across the snow, and steam wafted through the air as he sprinted down the street after Marvin.

"Daddy! Daddy, wait for me."

Rachel's mouth dropped open as she stared after her son. "What on earth—?"

"Daddy! Daddy, don't leave!" Danny screamed.

Rachel also dropped her cup as she tore after him. "Danny, come back!"

Wondering what had gotten into the boy, Sam followed at a slow lope.

Hearing the yells, Marvin paused just in front of the bank, turning to look over his shoulder. Danny tackled him, throwing his arms around Marvin's legs, almost knocking the man down. Marvin stumbled into a snowdrift, fighting to keep his balance, his eyes wide with surprise. He stared down at the child, his hands lifted in confusion. When he realized what happened, he reached down and patted Danny's shoulder. "I'm sorry, son, but I think you have the wrong daddy."

Danny looked up at Marvin's face and gaped in horror.

Recognition caused the child to instantly release the man. Danny staggered, shaking his head with disbelief, his mouth rounded, his wide eyes filled with tears.

Rachel dropped to her knees beside Danny, gripping his shoulders so she could turn him and look at his face. "Danny, you scared me to death."

Danny's chin quivered and he blinked, his small face contorted with despair. "You're not my daddy. I thought—" Danny choked back a sob as he buried his face against her shoulder. His body wrenched as his cries echoed down the street.

Tears filled Rachel's eyes. Sam's chest tightened and he couldn't take a deep breath. Ah, he hated seeing her and the boy cry.

"I'm sorry for the misunderstanding. I'm afraid he thought I was his father." Marvin's face reddened with embarrassment.

Rachel swallowed before her gaze moved over Marvin, her voice choked with emotion. "You…you're the right height and build, and Danny's father often wore a blue suit. He…he died a year ago. I'm so sorry for the trouble."

"Ah, I'm sorry to hear that." Genuine compassion covered Marvin's features.

Danny's desolate cries filled the crisp air. Sam's heart clenched as he patted the boy's shoulder. He'd also lost his father when he was young, and he wished he could do something to ease Danny's pain.

People along the street stopped to gawk. Sam didn't like them watching Rachel and her son when they were so vulnerable.

"No harm done." Marvin gave an uncomfortable smile before he turned and escaped inside the bank.

Rachel picked Danny up, cradling his gangly body against her as she packed him back to the truck.

"Can I carry him for you?" Sam offered.

She shook her head, tears trembling on her lashes. Sam

watched the scene as if from a bubble. He could see all the emotion playing out in front of him, yet he couldn't do a thing to help. He felt like an outsider and he didn't like it. For some insane reason, he longed to pick the boy up and make everything better.

"Shh, don't cry, sweetheart. I'm here," Rachel soothed, her cheek pressed against her child's.

Her voice cracked and so did Sam's heart. He followed her to the truck, helpless to do anything more than open the door and assist her as she climbed inside the cab with Danny in tow.

She sat huddled on the front seat with Danny in her lap, their heads close together. Sam got into the truck and turned on the engine before cranking up the heater. Because Danny wasn't wearing a seat belt, Sam didn't pull out into traffic. Instead, he clutched the steering wheel and stared out through the windshield. No one moved or spoke as Danny's cries subsided to soft shudders.

Rachel brushed at the dampness in her own eyes and Sam handed her the clean linen handkerchief he always kept in the left breast pocket of his shirt. She accepted it without a word, wiping Danny's tear-drenched cheeks before her own.

"You okay now?" she whispered against Danny's ear.

"Yes," the boy hiccuped, sounding miserable. He made no effort to move out of the safety of her arms as he rubbed his eyes with the backs of his hands.

"Mommy, are you gonna leave me, too?" Danny's bottom lip quivered, his eyes filling with fresh tears.

Sam looked away, his heart aching for Rachel and her little boy's loss. Parents should live to see their kids raised to adulthood.

"No, honey, I'll never leave you. The Lord has blessed us with so much. We're safe here in Finley, and I'll never let you go." She spoke fiercely, squeezing him tight, kissing his forehead and cheek.

Sam ran his fingers through his hair, thinking God could be so unfair. All these years, he'd felt sorry for himself because he'd lost Melanie five weeks before they were to be married. He'd cursed God many times for taking her. Not a day went by that he didn't remember and regret what he'd done to help cause that tragedy.

In spite of her loss, Rachel praised the Lord. Sam didn't understand how she could have so much faith.

"You think you can get back in your seat so we can go shopping now?" Rachel asked.

That brought a thin smile to the child's lips. He nodded but didn't say a word as he climbed into the backseat and stared out the window.

Sam passed his cup of lukewarm hot chocolate to the boy. "Hey, buddy. I can't drink this while I drive. Why don't you take it?"

When Sam looked at Rachel, she gave him a half-smile and mouthed the words *thank you.*

Sam's pulse beat a rapid tattoo. This woman made him feel all sorts of emotions he thought were long dead and buried. Anger, fear and compassion.

Jealousy.

And yet, offering her the job at his clinic was the right thing to do. He knew it deep in his bones. Still, as he drove to the hardware store, he had second thoughts. He must be crazy to bring her into his clinic. She'd be underfoot all day long, every day. He'd have to work with her constantly. He couldn't avoid her. Not anymore. He'd committed himself.

Later that morning, Sam carried Rachel's groceries inside her house, then stood with her and Danny out on the front porch. Blond curls framed her oval face, feminine and dainty.

Everything he was not.

He gestured toward his old clunker parked in her driveway. "You think you can drive that rig?"

"I guess so. Where do you want me to drive it to?"

He handed her the keys. "I thought you could use it, just until you get back on your feet and can afford something better."

Her eyes widened. "I can't accept this, Sam."

"Why not?"

"Because it's too much. It…it's your truck."

"I have two trucks. It's just a loan, Rach. Until you can get your own vehicle. You're gonna need a way to get into work every day. It's not much, but the heater works and she won't bottom out in mud or snow as long as you're careful."

Rach. Did she notice how he'd shortened her name? He had to keep reminding himself not to become too friendly with her. So far, it was proving almost impossible to distance himself from her and Danny.

He withdrew his gloves before digging into his coat pocket to pull out his cell phone. He reached for her hand and curled her fingers around the phone. Her skin felt soft but cold against his.

"What's this for?" she asked.

"Another perk of the job. If you're gonna work for me, you've got to have a phone."

She tried to hand the phone back to him. "No, absolutely not. I don't want any more handouts."

Handouts. Was that what this was? A niggling doubt inside his head warned him to run.

"I'll write it off as a business expense," he argued. "I've got to be able to reach you in case of an emergency at the clinic."

"An emergency?"

Not likely, but she didn't need to know that. He could buy another cell phone on his family plan with Gladys and write the cost off as a business expense. He should just leave her alone. The more he helped her, the more involved he would be in all aspects of her life. "Do you need a lesson on driving a stick shift?"

An impish smile crinkled her nose. "Nope. Grampy taught me to drive his tractor and truck, and I should do just fine."

He wasn't surprised. "Sounds like you'd make a good rancher's wife."

Now, why did he say that? She didn't respond and he felt his face heat with embarrassment. "Come in to work as soon as you get Danny registered for school. We open our doors at seven thirty, but I'll expect you in around nine. Danny can walk over to the clinic with Charlie when school gets out. I'll have chores for him to do until it's time to go home."

"I…I don't know what to say. Thank you. I'll be there."

"You're welcome." With a nod, he turned and walked down the steps and headed toward the gravel road.

"Wait! Can I drive you home?"

He pointed across the fields. "I can walk. I just live half a mile down the road. Call if you need anything. I've programmed my number into the phone."

He kept going, fearful she might refuse his gifts. Fearful she might call him on the phone and then hoping she did.

He glanced over his shoulder. She stood there watching him, looking small and fragile against the backdrop of her old, dilapidated farmhouse.

"You knucklehead!" Remembering how he'd told Rachel she'd make a good rancher's wife, he pressed the heel of his palm against his forehead. She probably thought he was flirting.

And maybe he was.

He shook his head, wondering why he was even thinking such thoughts. He couldn't become emotionally involved with Rachel. It was that simple.

Or was it?

He wanted to regret what he'd done, but he didn't. Instead, he lengthened his stride, filled with unexplainable joy. He'd see her tomorrow morning. In spite of his misgivings, he felt calm as a summer's morning.

Chapter Seven

The next day, Rachel registered Danny for school, then arrived at Sam's clinic just after nine a.m.

"Good morning," Gladys greeted her, as she stepped into the warm office.

Rachel caught the odor of wet dog and crinkled her nose.

"You can stow your purse and coat here." Gladys showed Rachel where to put her things, then pointed at the reception counter. "We call this the fishbowl. It's central to the office."

She led Rachel to the supply closet, then showed her the locked pharmacy cabinets, examination rooms, operating room, Sam's office and the kennels out back. For obvious reasons, the fishbowl divided the office for cats on one side and dogs on the other. The two examination rooms included doors on both sides, to admit felines or canines. Gladys explained procedures and tasks as they moved from room to room.

"Your main responsibility will be here at the reception desk. When we're busy, you'll help out with weighing the animals and taking them and their parents into the examination rooms."

Their parents. As in their owners. Rachel couldn't help being amused by the term.

Gladys showed her how to answer the phone and put calls on hold, how to schedule appointments, prepare invoices and create new patient files. Rachel ate it up, knowing she could do this with the Lord's help.

"Good morning," Sam greeted her as she directed the parent of one of their patients into an examination room. Sam wore a blue smock, his long legs wrapped in faded denim. His eyes glowed as he smiled at her and she felt all warm and happy inside.

By midmorning, she felt pretty sure of herself. She had a job working with nice people, and she even taught Gladys some shortcuts as they worked in the spreadsheet program. Gladys stayed by her side most of the day, training her on each new task and introducing her to the owners of their patients as they came in for appointments.

Except to deliver a chart or file to the examination rooms, Rachel saw very little of Sam. He stayed pretty busy taking care of patients. If the clientele didn't include dogs, Rachel thought her new job would be almost perfect.

Then the inevitable occurred. Gladys left Rachel to go back and assist Sam with a medical procedure. Rachel would have to fly solo.

She took a deep breath, prepared for anything. She'd come this far and overcome a lot of obstacles. Surely she could handle whatever walked through the door.

The little bell tinkled and the grumpiest-looking man she'd ever seen walked inside. In his arms he carried a mangy dog, its fur filled with burrs and stickers.

Rachel took a deep breath, determined to do the best job possible. She leaned her elbows on the counter, clutching her hands together as she smiled. "How can I help you?"

The man stepped up to the counter and thrust the dog into her arms. "Jack got outside again. Chased a rabbit through the sticker bushes. Needs Doc to fix him up."

Rachel came to her feet, almost dropping the dog. She stared in horror at the sad, black eyes barely visible beneath a matting of fur. The dog yelped in pain and she gasped. "Uh, do you have an appointment, sir?"

"Nope, this is an emergency. Just fix him up."

Filled with doubt, Rachel took a deep breath and shifted the dog's weight, trying to be patient. This animal looked like he needed a groomer, not a vet. "What…what's wrong with him?"

"Thorns in his paws. Doc will have to pull 'em out." The man walked over to a chair, picked up a magazine and slouched in his seat.

Taken aback, Rachel realized she was now out of her league. Dogs scared her to death, yet this animal was in obvious pain. If she didn't set the situation right, she might lose control. And she wanted to show Sam that she could work independently and take charge so he could care for the patients.

The dog whined and she flinched, panic climbing up her throat. What should she do?

Gladys came out of the examination room and reached for a package of gauze. She paused, staring at the reception area and Sam stepped over to the door. "What are you looking at?"

"Your new receptionist trying to cope with Bob Murdock."

Sam groaned. "Great! What is it this time?"

"Looks like Jack got into the sticker bushes again."

Sam poked his head out the door to see what was going on. He widened his eyes when he saw Rachel holding Jack, an expression of horror on her face as she stared at the scruffy-looking terrier.

"Rachel looks scared to death. Are you gonna step in and help her out?" he asked Gladys.

His sister folded her arms. "Nope."

He took a step, but Gladys stuck her arm out. "Let her learn, Sam. She can do this."

"One moment, sir." Rachel's voice quivered and Sam wondered at Gladys's wisdom. She'd seen Rachel's scars and he'd told her about Rachel's phobia for dogs.

He was about to push by his sister and intervene, but Rachel rounded the counter and carried the dog back to his owner. Bob Murdock stared at her in surprise.

Rachel wore a pleasant expression, seeming undaunted by Bob's surly frown. "If you'll tell me your name, I'll sign you in and let Dr. Thorne know you're here. Then you can take Jack into the examination room for care."

Bob's mouth dropped open and Sam held his breath. Old Bob Murdock wasn't used to anyone putting him in his place, even when done as nicely as Rachel had just treated him.

"Uh, the name's Bob Murdock. You must be new here."

"I am." She headed back around the counter where she opened a filing cabinet. She fingered through the files, withdrawing one manila folder. "Here you are. I'll let the doctor know you and Jack are here."

She turned to approach the examination room and saw Sam and Gladys watching her. Embarrassed to be caught staring, Gladys ducked away, but Sam couldn't move. Something held him prisoner, and he realized his respect for Rachel had just grown by leaps and bounds. She'd come a long way in just one day.

Her wide eyes told him she felt self-conscious, hoping for his approval. With one nod of his head, he winked at her. Rachel smiled, looking relieved and happier than he'd seen her since the day she arrived in town. He returned to the examination room and closed the door. Without saying a word, he'd just told her she was doing fine.

At lunchtime, Sam treated them each to a sandwich from

the diner. Needing to leave so she could speak with Martha Keller about the bazaar fund-raiser, Gladys offered to pick up the food. The boys would be out of school in several hours. Then, they'd come over to the clinic to feed, water and exercise the animals.

On his way to his office, Sam passed by the scale. He choked back a laugh as he watched Rachel trying to weigh Mrs. Cleary's poodle without touching the dog.

"Come on, get on." Rachel encouraged the mutt as she waved her hand toward the scale.

The animal stared up at her in blank confusion.

Rachel got down on her knees, making smooching sounds as she clicked her fingers to direct the dog onto the scale. "Come on, Princess. You can do it."

Princess lay down and rolled over, belly up, paws hanging limp in the air. The dog whined and gazed at Rachel submissively.

Sam couldn't resist. He bit back a laugh as he stepped up behind Rachel and leaned down, speaking low and deep. "You know, it might help if you pick the dog up and put her on the scale."

Rachel gasped in surprise and toddled backward, plopping onto the floor. "Sam, you startled me."

He chuckled and, shaking his head, turned and walked away. She still didn't like to handle the animals, but she was doing okay. He couldn't be more pleased with her progress.

Just before closing time, Sam found Rachel plowing through samples of dog food in the supply closet.

"What are you looking for?" he asked.

She drew back with a huff and pushed a curl of hair behind her ear. "I don't want to tell you."

Sam tilted his head to one side and tried not to smile. "Go on, humor me."

Rachel faced him, her hands on her hips. "Okay…where are the extra dog biscuits?"

Sam frowned. "Gladys just filled the jar up front yesterday."

"They're all gone."

"That supply should have lasted several days."

"Well, it didn't."

"So, what happened to them?"

Rachel gazed down at the floor and her shoulders sagged. "If I tell you the truth, promise you won't be upset?"

Sam braced himself. "They're only dog biscuits."

Rachel took a deep breath. "I've been using the biscuits to bribe the dogs and cats to get on the scale and follow me into the examination rooms."

"You're not kidding, are you?"

Ignoring her frown, Sam doubled over with a belly laugh. It took several seconds before he could catch his breath and respond. "There's a new bag in my office. Use all you need. We can always get more."

He hurried away before he let loose with more gales of laughter. If nothing else, Rachel's presence certainly provided comic relief in the office. He just hoped she didn't give all his patients a stomachache.

On Sunday morning, Rachel found another hundred-dollar bill taped behind the bathroom mirror. She figured she'd continue to discover more money in this old, drafty house. Dear old Grammy. How she loved and missed her.

Rachel drove Danny into town to Gladys's house so they could all go to church together. Sam picked them up at precisely a quarter to ten. Rachel had taken extra care with her hair and makeup, and wore her best Sunday dress; a feminine confection of lace and silk. Not really warm attire for such a cold winter's morning. Instead of high heels, she should be wearing warm boots, but vanity did crazy things to a woman. She wanted to make a good impression her first Sunday at church.

She couldn't explain the warm, tingly feeling as Sam's gaze traveled over her apparel. When he smiled with appreciation, she realized she'd accomplished her goal. And then she wondered why she cared if he approved of her appearance.

"Good morning. You find any more stashes of cash?" He teased, leaning against the doorjamb in Gladys' kitchen.

Likewise, she scanned his blue jeans, scruffy hat and scuffed cowboy boots, finding him too casual for church. Regardless, he looked good. Too good.

She looked away and reached for her coat and purse, trying to ignore the wave of heat flooding her neck and face. "Yes, but I never know when some money might turn up. Danny's birthday is coming up, so I've been glad for the extra money."

"Have you thought about a gift for him?"

"Yes. Before we moved here, he asked for a fire engine."

"I was wondering about a puppy. I have a brand new litter of black Labs out at my place and I thought—"

"No! Absolutely not. No dogs." She shook her head firmly.

"Danny! Charlie! We're leaving," Gladys yelled from the living room. "Don't forget we're going out to Sam's place for dinner after church."

The two boys came running and they all headed for the door. Gladys smoothed a rooster feather at the back of Charlie's head.

Sam chuckled and took Rachel's elbow before guiding her as she tottered down the treacherous steps. "Careful now. You don't want to twist an ankle in those stilts you're wearing."

She tensed but didn't pull away until he handed her up into the truck and she murmured her thanks. Gladys and the boys joined them and they buckled their seat belts.

When Sam pulled into the parking lot at the small red brick church, Gladys opened her door and hopped out with the two boys. Sam made no move to shut off the motor.

"You're not coming in?" Rachel asked.

He leaned his forearms on the steering wheel, looking straight ahead. "Nope."

I wish you'd change your mind.

The words stuck to the tip of her tongue. She felt sad to go to church without him, yet she couldn't explain why. The little she knew about this man made her feel like both a stranger and a confidante, and she couldn't decipher the feelings waging war inside her mind. "It might help. Going to church always brings me a peaceful feeling."

His gaze stabbed her. His frosty tone showed his true thoughts. "I'll pass, but thanks for your concern."

Okay, she could take a hint. No need for a sledgehammer between the eyes. Still, something unexplainable urged her to persist. The still, small voice of the Lord. "You know, the Savior told us to come unto Him and He would make our burdens light."

His eyes hardened. "And that's why so many God-fearing people don't have any problems, right?"

"No, we all have troubles, Sam. But relying on the Lord can make those burdens more bearable. He can ease our load."

He glared at her, his jaw locked. "You can keep your sermon to yourself. I'm not interested."

His words tore at her. "Oh, yes, I forgot. You don't need anyone, do you? You're fine all by yourself."

"That's right, hon. I like being alone," he snarled.

Hon! Who did he think he was speaking to? She opened her mouth to tell him what she thought of his rudeness, but then clamped her mouth shut. This was his hurt talking, nothing more. Instead, she decided on a different strategy.

"Okay, *babe*. Whatever you say." She laughed just to spite him before she slid out of the truck and closed the door.

As she picked her way across the slick sidewalk where someone had spread ice melt, she felt Sam's eyes drilling a hole in her back. She glanced over her shoulder and waved at him, catching his gaze upon her. He didn't even pretend not to stare, but she caught no resentment in his eyes. Instead, she saw a reflection of her own hidden pain.

Inside the building, Rachel recognized several people, some of whom she knew from when her grandparents had lived, and others she'd recently met over at the clinic. Organ music sifted over the air, creating a reverent environment.

Bill Sawyer, one of the elders in her congregation, shook her hand by the door. An old friend of her grandfather's, Bill had helped her make arrangements for Grammy's burial. "I was glad to hear you'd moved home. Myra would have liked having you here, living in her house."

Rachel bit her bottom lip. "I just wish I'd been here when she passed away."

"Well, you're here now. You call on us if you need anything." His round face and red cheeks creased with a smile.

Feeling welcomed, Rachel sat beside Gladys on a pew. She had to scold Danny only once, when he and Charlie became too irreverent. She was about to separate the two boys, who fought over ownership of a drinking straw Charlie had hidden in his pants pocket. The sermon on grief and losing someone you love captured Danny's attention. He listened intently to the dialogue on how the Savior can bring solace during such times of trial. His forehead creased with concentration, his mouth pursed tight. Rachel had never seen him so quiet in church before. This was what he needed. A friend like Charlie and someone besides his mother to tell him everything would be okay.

After Sunday school, Rachel joined Gladys in the front foyer, waiting for the boys to come out of their class. Gladys introduced her to several women, including Martha Keller, Shorty's wife. He stood close by, chatting with some other men about the snowmobiling activity planned in several weeks.

"Can we go, Mom? Can we, please?" Danny begged.

Rachel hesitated, not sure she liked the thought of her little boy riding on a machine that might crash and injure him…or worse. She didn't mean to be overprotective, but. Danny was all she had left. "We'll see."

"Ah, let him go. It'll be lots of fun, and we'll make sure he's safe," Shorty chimed in. Dressed in a gray suit, he looked completely different from the day he'd come out to her house to fill her propane tank. His booming laughter filled the room and she couldn't help smiling at his exuberance.

"You've come to Finley at a good time of year," Martha told her. "We're preparing for the annual bazaar fund-raiser. We'd be delighted if you can help out. I'm the chairwoman this year, and Susan's my cochairman." She pointed at another woman with long, soft curls the color of chestnuts.

"Hi! Welcome to Finley." Susan smiled, bouncing a toddler on her hip. "We're gonna have lots of booths and sell baked goods and all kinds of crafts."

Rachel felt overwhelmed. She'd never made crafts in her life. "I'm happy to help out, but I doubt I can contribute much."

"Can you sew?"

Rachel shook her head. "Not a bit."

"How about knit or crochet?"

Another shake. "I'm afraid all I do well is take pictures."

Rachel thought of the camera tucked inside her purse, a fresh roll of film always close at hand. She hated the new digital cameras. For some reason, she never actually printed those pictures, which meant they never found their way into her numerous photo albums. She loved the solitude of the darkroom where she developed her pictures. Photography had been the first class she took at the community college, and it proved both therapeutic and wonderful.

"Good! You can take some pictures around town, put them in frames and we'll sell them at the bazaar. This year, we're trying to earn enough money to pay for renovations on the old town hall. The building needs some serious electrical work." Martha turned her attention to her six-year-old, as if the matter of Rachel's help on the fund-raiser was all settled.

Rachel remained silent. Although she had a knack for finding unique shots, she wasn't a professional. She considered taking pictures a hobby, nothing more. She didn't even have access to a darkroom anymore. How could she do what they wanted?

When Sam picked them up after church, she mulled her dilemma over as they drove out to his place for Sunday dinner. Rachel kept her thoughts to herself. She wanted to immerse herself in her new community, but now she felt uncertain. She wasn't a crafty person and doubted she had much to offer at the fund-raiser.

The boys sat in the backseat, talking about the upcoming snowmobiling activity.

"I never been snowmobiling before," Danny told Charlie.

"You'll love it," Charlie said. "Uncle Sam has the best snowmobile in the county, don't you, Uncle Sam?"

Sam just smiled into the rearview mirror.

"He even let me drive it once all by myself. It's superfast," Charlie continued.

Rachel glanced back at her son as his eyes widened with awe. "Can I drive it, too?"

Sam cleared his throat, as if suppressing a chuckle. "We'll see."

"You'll have to learn how, first," Charlie said. "It's a machine you better respect or it could take your life."

Rachel hid a smile. No doubt Charlie quoted Sam after he'd warned his nephew of the dangers. If Sam were driving, Rachel didn't think she'd mind Danny going on the activity. And then she realized something that left her stunned. Her feelings for Sam had changed over the past week since she came to town. He was her boss, but also her friend. She'd never planned to trust and rely on him, but she did.

When they pulled into Sam's driveway, they all piled out of the truck. Gladys handed a plastic bag of groceries to each of the boys.

"I'll be in as soon as the livestock are fed." Sam headed for the barn while they went inside the house.

In the laundry room, two baskets of dirty clothes rested beside the washing machine. Shiny oak floors gleamed in the rambling country kitchen. A bridle hung on the back doorknob, and a pair of spurs lay beside the door. Somehow the slight disorder made Sam seem more human, and completely masculine.

Rachel stared at the stainless-steel appliances, the marble-slab countertops, the double ovens, and the king-sized refrigerator. "No wonder you like to cook in this kitchen."

Gladys nodded and heaved a sigh of bliss. "Yeah, it's purty, isn't it? I love this kitchen."

Rachel agreed. As she picked up a bag of potatoes and began peeling them, she felt strangely happy and content working in Sam's kitchen.

Later, she went to the refrigerator for a stick of butter and peeked into the living room. She stared, awed by the beautiful rock fireplace filling one entire wall. A variety of framed photographs rested on the high mantel. Beautiful artwork of mountain scenes and green forests decorated the walls. Comfy leather sofas and chairs sat in an intimate group around an oak coffee table.

Nothing but the best.

The back door rattled and Sam came inside, grinning as he doffed his muddy boots and coat. "You finding what you need?"

Startled, Rachel grabbed for the fridge door, ducking her head inside.

"We're doing fine. Did you get the horses fed?" Gladys asked.

"I did. I have Carl Newton's prize mare in the barn, sick with colic." He stood at the sink in the utility room, washing his hands.

"Again? Every winter, you have one of his horses in your barn. Did you remind him to break the ice over his troughs so his animals can drink?" Gladys didn't look up as she placed the ham in a pan.

"Yeah, I reminded him."

As he dried his hands on a clean towel, Sam's eyes locked with Rachel's. His presence made her jittery and her hands shook as she unwrapped the butter.

He sauntered across the room to peer over her shoulder. "What you making?"

"Au gratin potatoes." His nearness caused butterflies to dance in her stomach.

He reached for a carrot stick and bit into it, munching as he perused their work. "Mmm, smells good, ladies. You need any help?"

"Not yet, but as soon as we have the ham cooked, you can slice the meat."

"You got it."

"Uncle Sam!" Charlie ran down the hall and headed straight for his uncle, throwing his arms around Sam's long legs.

"Ooff! Hi, buddy!" Sam swooped the boy high into the air.

Danny joined them, laughing as both boys tackled the big

man. Sam picked up Danny, and the boys squealed and bumped into the table. A bowl clattered to the floor.

"Shoo!" Gladys ordered. "Go somewhere else to play. Good thing it was plastic."

"Can I go out to the barn, Sam?" Danny hopped up and down. "I want to see your new puppies."

"Sure, but stay away from the corrals, boys. I've got a cow out there recovering from milk fever and I don't want you to disturb her."

"Okay! Come on, let's go, Charlie."

Both boys skidded to the door, plopping onto the floor to pull on their rubber boots. Still chuckling, Sam padded across the floor in his socks and disappeared into the family room. The sounds of a football game blaring on the big-screen TV soon filtered over the air.

Gladys shook her head and chuckled. "You see what I mean? We've got three boys to raise." She rinsed a head of lettuce before handing it to Rachel to cut up for the salad. "It's nice having you and Danny here. Charlie loves having another new playmate."

"Danny's happy, too. It's good to hear him laugh again." Rachel measured out cornstarch to thicken the glaze for the ham, remembering joyous meals spent with Alex. She longed to feel that way again.

"So, what do you think of Sam's house?"

Gladys's question took Rachel off guard, and she glanced at the doorway. With the noise from the football game, she doubted he could hear them. "I think it's absolutely beautiful."

"He built most of it himself. Took him three years. There's not much that man can't do around the house. Although I have no idea why he built such a fancy kitchen. He can't cook at all. He eats most of his meals over at my place after work."

She chuckled as she rinsed two ripe tomatoes and placed them on the chopping block.

Rachel stared at the oak table surrounded by a lovely bay alcove. "Maybe one day his wife will make good use of this kitchen."

Gladys snorted. "I wish he'd get married. But he doesn't seem interested."

"You got any apple pie?"

Sam entered the room and both Rachel and Gladys flinched. He shamelessly dipped his finger into a fruit salad, then stuck a piece of orange in his mouth. Gladys gasped and slapped his hand before he reached to open the fridge. His upper torso disappeared inside as he searched for what he wanted. He soon emerged with a tin of homemade apple pie.

"You're gonna ruin your dinner," Gladys scolded.

He grinned. "Not a chance."

Whipping the dish towel from over her shoulder, Gladys snapped it at him. When he lunged for her, she giggled and evaded him by running around the island in the middle of the kitchen. His deep laughter filled the room as he chased after his sister. He came up short in front of Rachel, no more than a handsbreadth apart as he smiled down into her eyes.

"Hiding behind Rachel won't save you, sis. I can take on both of you." His words were for Gladys, but his eyes burned into Rachel's. A lopsided smile curved his handsome mouth, deepening the dimple in his cheek. She met his gaze, unable to resist the pull of his magnetic charm.

"Wait a minute. I'm innocent." Entranced by their play, Rachel held up her hands to ward him off.

He lifted one brow in skepticism. "Yeah, you're innocent with that sweet little smile of yours. You're as innocent as a snake in the grass."

"What did I do?" she asked, trying her best not to laugh.

"I remember your grandpa being mighty upset after you got the crazy notion to repair the broken planks on the dock over at the duck pond. You put his toolbox in the boat, then untied the rope. While you got sidetracked picking field flowers, the boat floated out to the middle of the pond."

Her face heated with embarrassment. She'd been ten years old at the time. "He told you about that?"

"Who do you think he sent out into the pond to retrieve the boat?"

"Oh," she groaned, covering her face with one hand. She remembered a young cowhand being sent by her grandfather to fetch the boat and expensive toolbox. Before he swam out to the middle of the pond, the man had removed his shirt, hat and boots, then spent the rest of the day slogging around the fields in wet blue jeans. That young man had been Sam.

"It's a good story for blackmail if I ever want something from you. Just remember that, lady." He winked at her in warning before reaching for a fork. "Now, I'm going back to my game. I love having Danny around. He keeps Charlie occupied so I don't have to do any jigsaw puzzles while I watch football."

"Oh, you!" Gladys snapped her towel again.

With no idea of the warm impact his words had on Rachel, he chuckled and returned to the living room with his pie. Looking up, Rachel saw Gladys staring at her with an odd expression.

"What?" Rachel asked.

"Well, I'll be." The woman lifted a hand to rest on her hip. "I sensed it at the clinic, but I wasn't quite sure. Now, I see it clear as day."

"I don't understand." Rachel turned and picked up the can opener and proceeded to open a can of yams.

The whir of the motor didn't deter Gladys, who gave Rachel a hug. "Honey, I'm sure glad you're here. I never thought Sam would look at another woman again, but I guess I was wrong."

"What do you mean?"

Sam returned to the kitchen, making a beeline for the refrigerator. "I forgot the whipped cream. Can't have pie without whipped cream."

He smiled and waggled his eyebrows at Rachel before taking out a large bowl of freshly whipped cream and setting it on the kitchen counter. With a few stiff movements, he pulled back the plastic wrap, scooped a generous portion of cream onto his pie, returned the bowl to the fridge, then hurried back to the family room. As he passed by, he reached out and tugged on the ties of Rachel's apron so they came undone.

"You scat, varmint!" She laughed as she retied her apron strings, feeling warm and funny inside. When she glanced at Gladys, the other woman leaned against the counter and folded her arms in an I-told-you-so manner.

"What?" Rachel asked, her cheeks burning with heat.

"He hasn't smiled or teased another woman like that since—" She broke off the sentence, as if she were about to say something but then thought better of it.

"Since what?"

"Oh, nothing. But you've gotten under his skin, my dear, and I like the change in him. He's happier than he's been in years."

Rachel didn't want to get under any man's skin. Sam wasn't Alex. And yet, the more she tried to remind herself of that fact, the more she resented it. She loved and missed her husband, but Sam made her forget her sadness. He made her want to live again.

Turning away, she reached for the hot pads, slipping them onto her hands before she opened the oven and removed a pan of fluffy rolls. She would ignore Gladys and her innuendoes. She and Sam worked together, nothing more.

Who was she kidding? She didn't understand what was going on between them, but she knew her feelings toward the handsome doctor were anything but remote.

She hardened her eyes, determined not to let her feelings run rampant. She had to think of Danny and protect the fragile peace they'd found here in Finley. She had to protect her heart.

Chapter Eight

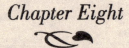

After dropping Gladys and Charlie off at their house, he drove to Hillside Cemetery and parked his truck beneath the tall evergreens lining the lane on the west side.

Like every Sunday evening, he would drive over to the clinic and feed the animals boarding there before he went back home. But today had been different. Rachel and Danny had joined them in their meal.

He remembered Rachel wearing one of Gladys's checkered aprons. Helping prepare the meal, setting the table in his dining room with Gladys's best china.

Sam couldn't explain the buzz of excitement he felt as he thought about having Rachel in his home, enjoying the afternoon with him and the boys. Even after spending the afternoon with her, he still wanted to see her again. To know he hadn't dreamed her into his life. He'd spent the past twelve years building his practice and hiding from his own feelings. Deep inside, he knew he needed more. And Rachel Walker was just what he needed.

Opening the door to his truck, Sam stepped out and skirted a large mud puddle. As he stepped onto the grass, his gaze scanned the tops of the surrounding headstones, their bases buried in crusted snow. He knew this cemetery by heart. Many of the people buried here were friends or relatives. As a child, he'd loved coming here on Memorial Day, placing dandelions on his grandmother's grave and climbing trees so he could look out over the entire cemetery…until Gladys scolded him for being irreverent.

He paused before a grave, the flat headstone obscured in the frozen ground. Bending at the waist, he brushed the snow away. His fingers caressed the block letters etched in the cold marble. He stood straight and stared down at the white stone, placing his frozen hands into his pants pockets. A chilling breeze swept the glade and he hunched his shoulders, wishing he'd worn a warmer coat.

Why did he come here today? He wanted to feel happy. To give thanks and be grateful for all the blessings in his life. Gratitude wasn't an emotion he felt much anymore. His mother taught him that grateful people were happier people, but he didn't feel very grateful. Not to the Lord. Not to anybody. He just felt empty and alone.

Guilt weighed him down like a ten-ton sledge. Memories flooded his mind as he thought of all the things he wished he'd said to Melanie while he had the chance. He also wished he could take back his harsh words. He could never forget or forgive himself for what he'd done, and he had no doubt the Lord would never forgive him, either. If only he had two minutes to apologize to Melanie, to keep her calm until he could stop the car, she might be alive today. They never would have married, but he wouldn't be haunted by her death now.

A tear ran down his cheek and he brushed it away before it froze to his skin. What would Rachel say if she saw him crying like a big baby?

Thinking of Rachel sobered him like nothing else could. He didn't understand why her opinion mattered. Or why he couldn't get the blue-eyed beauty off his mind. He'd always been a sucker for women in trouble. He tried to tell himself that was why he felt so drawn to Rachel. But in his heart, he knew the truth went much deeper than that. A part of him wanted to try and make up for what he'd done by helping others when he could. Now seemed like a good time to put his desires into action.

Something about Rachel touched him like no one else could. Her forthright courage even though she was afraid. Her dedication to her young child. Her gentle beauty and the way her nose crinkled when she laughed. Her sweet voice when she reasoned with her son. The funny way she used one finger to pet the animals at the clinic. Everything about her drew him like the ocean to the shore.

He stood there surrounded by barren maple trees, his feet cold in the snow, his heart empty, his conscience heavy as lead. He didn't realize how miserable and lonely he'd been all these years. Not until Rachel came into his life.

Rachel awakened in the middle of the night to find a small form standing beside her bed. She glanced at the clock on the nightstand. Three fifteen in the morning.

"Mommy?"

"Danny, what is it? Is something wrong?" She sat up, peering through the darkness at his small face.

"I had a bad dream."

She heard the tears in his voice and reached for him. "Oh, it's okay, baby."

He wrapped his small arms around her and she pulled him into bed with her, cuddling him beneath the covers. He smelled sweet from his bubble bath. As they lay on her pillow, their heads touched and she rubbed his arms in soothing caresses. It felt good to know he was here and safe.

"You want to tell me about your dream?"

She felt him shake his head. "No. It was 'bout Daddy. He was on a boat out in the water, leaving us behind. I couldn't get to him, and he wouldn't come back. I kept yelling at him not to leave us, but he didn't listen. Then, I snorted and woke up."

She swallowed a laugh and kissed his forehead, holding him tighter. "It was just a dream, sweetie. Daddy would never leave us on purpose. He loved us very much."

He sniffled. "Then why did he go away? Did I do something bad?"

"No! It wasn't your fault. It wasn't anyone's fault. His body just couldn't keep living anymore. But he never wanted to leave us."

While she fought the burn of tears, Danny remained silent for several minutes. She couldn't see his face and thought he must have fallen asleep.

"Mom?" He sounded drowsy.

"Yes."

"I miss Daddy something awful. Sometimes I can't remember what he looks like."

Her heart squeezed. How she wished she could take away his pain. "I know, sweetheart. I miss him something awful, too. I'll get you a picture to keep by your bed, so you'll never forget what he looks like, okay?"

"Yeah. Do you think we'll ever see him again?"

"Yes, we're a forever family."

"How do you know?"

She placed his hand over her heart. "I know it in here. Nothing will ever break our family apart. Not even death."

A long pause followed and then a yawn. "Do you like Sam?"

She hesitated, wondering where this conversation was

going. "Of course I like him. He's a very nice man and he's been very kind to us."

"Yeah, I think so, too. But he's not my dad."

A curious observation. "No one can ever replace your father."

"How come Daddy never played in the snow with us like Sam does?"

Rachel took a deep breath, wondering how to explain her husband's difficult upbringing. "Daddy was different from Sam. Your father grew up in a different world, with different parents and different expectations. But remember how Daddy barbecued hot dogs for us? And remember how he took you to the zoo? Your father was a good man. He worked hard to provide for us, and he never went to bed without kissing you good-night, even after you'd fallen asleep."

"Yeah, I remember." She could hear the smile in his voice and he gave a sleepy giggle. "Daddy sure loved us, didn't he?"

"Yes, he did." She pulled the blankets tighter around his shoulders. "Now, go to sleep and don't worry about a thing. We're gonna be just fine here in Finley."

"I know. And I got a friend already. Charlie and I are best buds. He even told the other kids at school."

She laughed. "I'm glad. Good friends are hard to find."

He smothered a big yawn with his hand. "Mom?"

"Hmm?"

"I'm gonna take care of you. I'm the man of the house, now Dad's gone, and I won't let you down." He snuggled closer and she couldn't believe how mature he sounded for his years.

She laughed and gave him a squeeze. "Daniel Walker, I love you so much. You're such a good boy and I'm proud of you. How'd you get to be so smart?"

She felt his little shrug. "Daddy taught me. I want to be an accountant like him when I grow up."

A lump as big as Kansas formed in her throat. She took a

deep, settling breath and released it. "You can choose whatever you want to be, but remember without the Lord in your life, you're nothing. No success can compensate for failure in your own home."

She wondered: if Alex could change things before he died, would he have spent more time with her and Danny, or would he have spent more time working at the office? She knew the answer, but she regretted that she and Alex would never have a second chance to spend more time together in this life.

"I'll remember, Mom." Conviction filled his voice. His fingers curled around the blanket and she felt him relax. Soon, his breathing deepened and she knew he slept.

She held him close, breathing deeply of his warm, sweet skin, relishing this moment. One day, he'd be all grown up and too embarrassed to let her hold him like this. She imagined the years would pass much too quickly. But right now, she had her little boy safe in her arms, and this memory would last her a lifetime.

The next afternoon at the clinic, Rachel went through her routine as usual. She called to remind people of their appointments for tomorrow, sorted the accounts and prepared the billings.

Three patients were waiting in the reception room to see the doctor when Lucille Garvey burst through the door. Lucille had been Grammy's best friend, and Rachel remembered eating homemade chocolate chip cookies over at the woman's house. Now, streaks of tears marred Lucille's powdered cheeks, and her gray hair was matted on one side. Runs striped her nylons, her knees black and scratched from kneeling in the dirt. In her thin arms, she cradled Morty, her red-and-white basset hound, who was wrapped in bloody towels.

"Oh, please help me. Please!" Lucille cried, as she rushed up to the front counter.

Rachel came out of her seat. "What happened?"

"He got out of the yard. I finally found him up on the interstate. He…he must have been hit by a car." Lucille's voice vibrated with hysteria.

Rachel didn't think before she took Morty into her arms. The dog gave several shrill yelps, in obvious pain. She cradled him against her chest, grateful for the blue smock she wore to protect her clothes from animal hair and blood.

"Come with me." Ignoring the other patients, Rachel carried Morty, using her shoulder to push past the swinging doors to the back of the clinic.

Lucille followed, sobbing and wringing her hands. Her crinkled face contorted in a mask of anguish. "It's all my fault. Please help him. Now your grandma's gone, he's all I have left in the world. I can't lose him. I just can't."

They met Sam in the back room, laughing as he pressed a stethoscope to the side of Mr. Hangton's orange tabby cat. The minute he saw them, Sam's smile faded and he handed the cat over to Gladys. "I'm sorry, Tom, but I've got an emergency."

"Of course. Take care of Morty." Tom stepped aside, his forehead furrowed with concern as he watched Sam usher Rachel into the surgical room.

"What happened?" he asked, completely focused on Morty.

The dog cried as Sam took the animal from Rachel and laid him on the steel operating table. Lucille was too upset to speak, so Rachel explained.

As Sam folded back the towels to see the injuries, the dog struggled, yelping and whimpering. The pitiful sounds made Rachel want to weep, but she knew she must be strong right now.

She held Morty's head, careful not to let the animal bite

her in an act of self-defense. In his pain, the dog had no idea they were trying to help him.

Rachel pressed the animal down, gentle but firm, while Sam examined the wounds. The dog's right front leg had been skinned, the leg broken and mangled. Rachel bit her bottom lip, wanting to run away, but unable to desert this helpless animal.

"Can you help him?" Lucille asked behind them.

"I'm sure gonna try, Lucille." Sam didn't look at her while he spoke. Instead, he talked to the dog in a soothing monotone as he determined further injuries. "There, Morty. Yes, I know it hurts. Don't worry, we're gonna fix you up."

Gladys appeared with a hypodermic. She held the dog still while Sam administered the sedative. With Gladys there to assist, Rachel stepped back, discovering blood on her hands. She quickly washed, changed her stained smock, then wrapped her arm around Lucille's waist. "Why don't we wait in Dr. Thorne's office while he takes care of Morty?"

"Is he gonna be okay?" Lucille stared over her shoulder at Morty, her eyes filled with fear.

Rachel's heart wrenched. Lucille lived all alone, with no one in the world except her congregation at church to care for her, not even a distant relative. Rachel understood what this little dog meant to the elderly lady. If Grammy had lived with a dog, would she still be alive today? Animals could provide so much companionship and love. Rachel wanted to promise that Morty would be fine, but she didn't dare. Not until Sam could determine the extent of his injuries. "You know Dr. Thorne will do everything in his power to save Morty. When did you get him?"

"Seven years ago. Dr. Thorne got him for me after I had a stroke. So I wouldn't be all alone if I fell."

"What a nice gesture. How long have you lived here in Finley?" Rachel kept up a steady stream of chatter, to take

Lucille's mind off Morty. Her strategy seemed to work, and the woman calmed some.

After sitting Lucille in a comfortable chair in Sam's office, Rachel got her a cup of water and a box of tissues. She then made a quick trip to the reception room, where she warned the other patients the doctor might be tied up for a while. "I'm sorry for the inconvenience. If you want to reschedule, I'm happy to do that for you, or you're welcome to wait."

"I'll wait, just to make sure Morty's okay. I know how I'd feel if it were my dog," Clarice Wells said. Her leashed golden retriever lay panting at her feet.

"Poor Lucille must be beside herself." Tom Hangton hovered by the front door, seeming reluctant to leave.

"I'll be back in a minute. I want to check on Lucille." Rachel returned to Sam's office, not wanting to leave the woman alone for very long.

The next two hours passed quickly. Rachel moved back and forth between the front reception room and the back office. Several times, Lucille stood and paced outside the surgical room, peeking through the glass windows to see that Sam and Gladys were still in the middle of surgery. Finally, Lucille went out front to find comfort from her friends.

"If Morty dies, I don't know what I'll do," she told them over and over again. They hugged and reassured her, and Rachel found herself in awe of their kindness.

Rachel also fretted over the little dog's well-being. She offered a silent prayer, asking the Lord to help guide Sam so he could mend Morty's broken body.

When Charlie and Danny came in from school, she cautioned them to be extra quiet as they went about their chores. Though he'd never met the dog, Danny seemed upset by the news, standing on a chair so he could peer through the glass at Sam.

"Is Morty gonna be okay, Mom?" he asked, his little chin quivering.

She gave him a comforting hug. "I hope so. Why don't you say a prayer for him?"

"I prayed for Daddy to come home, but it didn't help."

Rachel stared at her son, dumbstruck. "But Daddy was already gone by the time we found out. Our prayers should have been for ourselves then."

He clenched his jaw, looking so much like his father that she wanted to cry. She hated the thought that he didn't believe God answered his prayers. As she took hold of one of his hands, she sat on a chair and looked into his eyes. "Honey, sometimes we pray, but that doesn't mean God will give us what we want. He knows what's best for us, what will make us grow and learn to walk in faith. He answers our prayers in His time, not ours."

Danny's eyes welled up. "So, when can Daddy come home?"

She felt as though someone stabbed her heart. Tears burned the backs of her eyes. "He *is* home, honey. And one day we'll join him in heaven. I know it."

His eyes narrowed with disbelief and he jerked away. She would have called him back, but he ran out to join Charlie at the kennels. Most days, she thought he handled his grief pretty well. But at times like this, she feared what he might be thinking and how difficult the death of his father might prove to be for him throughout his life. How she wished she could give his father back to him. She prayed God would give her son the strength he needed to face life without his daddy. He just needed time to come to understand that his father wasn't coming home…a difficult lesson for a small child.

As Rachel returned to her desk, her heart felt leaden with despair. She tried to concentrate on her work when something furry startled her and she looked down. Tom's cat twined its body around her legs, purring. The feline jumped up on the counter, looking at her with glowing eyes. Unable to fight the impulse, Rachel smiled and petted the animal on the head.

Closing time came and went. Rachel gave the boys granola bars she had slipped into her purse that morning. She hoped they would satisfy the boys' hunger until they could get some real dinner.

Darkness fell and the streetlight outside came on, shining down on the damp sidewalk below. Rachel didn't lock the front door or close the blinds. Word of Morty's accident spread via cell phone, and several more people came to wait with Lucille in the reception room.

Sam startled them when he came up front, his surgical mask hanging loose about his neck. He pulled the surgical cap off his head while everyone in the room stared at him with expectancy. He took a deep breath, his shoulders slumped with fatigue. Lucille pressed her hands against her mouth, waiting for him to speak.

Sam squeezed Lucille's arm, his eyes filled with compassion. "You can stop worrying. Morty's gonna be just fine. His leg's broken and he'll be laid up for some time, but he should walk again."

The people in the room cheered. Lucille melted into fresh sobbing. "Oh, thank you, thank you, Dr. Thorne. I won't let him outside alone ever again. I promise."

"Nah, it's good for dogs to romp around outside. How about if I just come over next week and mend your fence. Then you can let him out in the yard without worry."

"You don't need to do that, Dr. Thorne."

"Yeah, I do." He gave her a kind smile and rubbed her back. His generosity toward the elderly lady touched Rachel's heart.

Lucille hugged Sam, gasping with relief as she dabbed her eyes with a tissue. Over her head, Sam's gaze locked with

Rachel's. In his eyes, she saw his approval and his appreciation. He winked at her and her insides melted. For the first time since Alex had died, she felt like she belonged, was a part of something unique and wonderful.

"Can…can I see Morty?" Lucille asked.

"Of course. Come on." Sam led her to the back room, speaking in a low tone. "He'll need to stay here overnight, just so I can keep an eye on him. I'll give you some pain medication when he goes home."

Their voices faded and Rachel faced the people in the reception room. They smiled, and she heard the relief in their happy voices as they laughed and hugged one another. And then she realized Sam wasn't just the town vet. He also helped bring these people together as a community. "Okay, folks, Morty's gonna be fine and it's time for me to close up shop."

"Wow! Look at the time. I've got to get home," Clarice said.

"Thanks for letting us stay, Rachel." Tom picked up his tabby and wrapped his coat around the chubby animal.

"You're welcome." She ushered them out the door, waving goodbye.

Danny burst into the reception room, a huge smile on his face. "Mom! Did you hear? Morty's gonna be okay."

"Yes, sweetheart, I heard. You see? God does answer our prayers."

Danny looked at the floor, his brows knit together as he thought this over. When he looked up at her, she saw deep sadness in his eyes. "I guess you're right, but I sure miss Daddy."

"I'm glad. That means you loved him. I miss him, too."

He smiled and gave her a hug before racing back to the surgery room.

As Rachel locked the front door, a thought caused her to pause. She'd cradled Morty in her arms like an injured baby. In her efforts to help others, she'd forgotten her own fears.

She thought of how Sam handled the situation. His kindness to Lucille, his gentle but hurried skill in dealing with Morty's wounds. Her respect for Sam Thorne grew by leaps and bounds.

Chapter Nine

That night, after Rachel and Danny left the clinic, she drove down the dark Main Street. Lamplight showed not another person in sight. As they passed the diner, she noticed the absence of Dwayne Claridge's truck in the parking lot. He wasn't working tonight and she had a fun idea. "You want to have dinner at the café tonight? I don't feel like cooking and they don't close for another forty minutes."

"Yay! Can I have a cheeseburger?" Danny bounced up and down on his seat.

"Of course." She pulled a U-turn and parked the clunker at the side of the building.

Inside the warm diner, the bell tinkled above the door as they entered and seated themselves in one of the booths. With the late hour, they had the place to themselves.

A young woman wearing a pink waitress uniform and carrying a notepad came out to wait on them. "Hi there. I'm Cherise. Do you already know what you want?"

"I think so. Do you still make chocolate-marshmallow milkshakes?" Rachel asked.

Cherise cracked the gum inside her mouth and smiled. "Sure."

"We'll have two milkshakes and two cheeseburgers with steak fries."

Cherise jotted some notes on her pad. "Coming right up."

She whirled around and headed for the kitchen, where she put their order up on a clip for the cook. The phone on the wall rang and Cherise answered it, writing down an order to go. "Okay, we'll have your food ready when you arrive."

Ten minutes later, Rachel and Danny sipped their milkshakes while they waited for their meal.

"Mmm, this brings back memories," Rachel told her son, as she stirred her milkshake with her straw.

"What kind of memories?" He smiled, looking pleased with his treat.

"Good ones. Grammy and Grampy used to bring me here and bought me chocolate-marshmallow shakes when I was a kid your age."

"Really?"

"Yes, and we ordered burgers and steak fries with fry sauce, just like we're having tonight."

Danny beamed happily, and she leaned across the table to wipe a dribble of milkshake from his chin. Rachel realized they were now making new memories for him to cherish.

Cherise brought them their food, placing two red baskets of thick fries beside their cheeseburgers. "Here you go. Enjoy!"

The bell over the door tinkled and Sam Thorne walked in.

"Hey! There's Sam." Danny pointed at the tall man.

"Hi, Sam! I've got your order ready." Cherise hurried off to the kitchen.

Sam saw Rachel and Danny and immediately sauntered over to their booth. "Looks like you had the same idea as me. A bit late to go home and scrounge up something for dinner."

"Will you join us?" Rachel offered, prepared to scoot over and let him sit next to her.

"I'd love to, but I ordered my food to go. I need to get home and feed my livestock."

"I got a chocolate-marshmallow milkshake." Danny held up the cup. "Mom says it tastes like Grammy and Grampy."

A quizzical expression crossed Sam's face and he chuckled as he looked at Rachel. "It tastes like your grandparents?"

"No, silly. It doesn't taste like them; it *reminds* me of them," Rachel corrected with a laugh.

Cherise came out of the kitchen carrying a brown paper sack. She clasped Sam's arm and gave him a sickeningly sweet smile. "Here you go, honey. I put extra fry sauce inside, just the way you like it."

Sam took the bag and stepped back, but Cherise lingered close by his side. Did he have feelings for the woman? His body language told her no, but the way Cherise hovered over him bothered Rachel. A pang of jealousy twisted inside her as she watched him withdraw his wallet and hand some bills to the waitress. Rachel couldn't explain her sudden emotions.

"See you tomorrow?" Sam smiled at Rachel.

She nodded. "Like always."

"Take it easy, champ." He ruffled Danny's hair, then turned and left.

Cherise followed behind, standing at the window as she watched him go. Rachel heard his truck pull away from the café, and Cherise heaved a giant sigh. "Mmm, that man has got it all."

"What does she mean, Mommy?" Danny whispered loudly as Cherise retrieved two decanters and sat at a table, filling the salt and pepper shakers.

Rachel shrugged, trying to sound normal. "I guess she likes Sam."

The boy stared at the door, a frown tugging at his mouth. "I like him, too, but he's not Daddy."

No, he wasn't Alex, and Rachel found herself wishing he were. This was the second time Danny had made this observation, almost as if he feared Sam might try to take his father's place. The fact that he liked Sam gave her an inkling of hope. And yet, Danny's feelings were just one more reinforcement why she shouldn't be interested in the handsome doctor.

Somehow the magic of the evening had dwindled and they finished their food and left. As they drove home, Rachel had never felt so lonely in all her life.

"I'm cold, Mommy." Danny stood at the top of the stairs to the basement, pulling on another sweatshirt over top of his Rocketman jammies.

"I know, honey. Bundle up until bedtime. I'll see what can be done." Rachel stood down in the coal room, spraying the beam of her flashlight across the old furnace. She had no idea how to troubleshoot the problem.

Even with the extra cash she'd found hidden around the house, she couldn't afford to buy a new furnace right now. She thought of calling Shorty, hating the thoughts of making him come out this late at night. Instead, she went upstairs and called Sam, just to ask if he could tell her what to do.

"I'll be right over," he said.

"But I don't want you to—"

Too late. He'd hung up. Within ten minutes, his truck pulled into her front yard. When he rapped his knuckles on the front door, she opened, her face heated with embarrassment. "I didn't mean for you to come over here. I thought maybe you could just tell me what to do."

"It's no trouble." He flashed a grin as he wiped his feet on the doormat, then removed his hat and stepped into the living room.

"Howdy, partner," Sam called to Danny, who sat huddled beneath a heavy quilt on the sofa, watching TV.

"Hi," Danny returned in a monotone.

"I think I'll check your pilot light and thermocouple." Sam walked into the kitchen and inclined his head toward the back stairs.

"Thermo-what?" Rachel squinted her eyes in confusion.

"Thermocouple. It detects heat and cold and connects the thermostat to the furnace. It may need to be replaced." He headed for the basement.

Rachel watched him go, finding his presence comforting. It almost seemed as though he belonged here. Then, she reminded herself that Danny didn't want another father and she still loved Alex.

Flipping on the light switch at the top of the stairs, Sam gazed through the dim gloom before walking down the narrow steps to the basement. Like many farmhouses built in the 1930s, this had once been a coal room before being converted into a utility room.

He stooped so he wouldn't bump his head on the low beams of lumber. He found the furnace tucked back behind the old coal chute. As he pulled the thin flashlight from the chain hung on his belt loop, he clicked it on and held it between his teeth, spraying light in front of him so he could see better. Ducking down, he peered in at the pilot light. Yep! The light was out. A little breeze was all it took in this drafty house.

He reached into his pants pocket and pulled out a book of matches he'd put there just for this purpose. Bending down, he lit the pilot light and watched until it gleamed bright red before he shook the match out.

"Need any help?"

Conk! He brought his head up too fast and banged it against the coal chute. The flashlight fell from between his teeth and clattered to the cement floor.

"Ouch!" He rubbed the back of his head, biting his tongue to keep from uttering a foul word. Somehow he knew Rachel wouldn't approve. He couldn't explain why her opinion mattered, but it did. He wanted to make her happy. More than anything else in the world. And that left him stumped. Since when did he care about pleasing a woman? Never! Not even Melanie.

She stood in the shadows, waving another flashlight, its beam nearly blinding him. Raising his arm, he shielded his eyes from the piercing light. "No, I think I've got it."

As he picked up the flashlight he'd dropped and stood to his full six feet and four inches, her chin tilted and she backed up a step. He didn't want her to be frightened of him.

"Let me show you the problem." He pointed out the pilot light and showed her how to light it in the future.

"Thank you. I'm sorry you had to come over here for such a trivial thing."

"I don't mind." He spoke the truth. It delighted him that she had called on him in times of trouble. As though she trusted him.

She glanced about the dark room and shivered, wrapping one arm around herself. "Brrr! It's cold. I've hated coming down here ever since I was a child."

He doffed his jacket and dropped it over her shoulders. She smiled her thanks, and his heart melted. As long as he lived, he'd never understand why he felt so happy in this woman's presence. Like he could conquer the world.

"What were you afraid of?" He thought of her as a small girl, frightened of the dark cellar.

She shrugged. "Mostly spiders. It's creepy down here."

He peered through the shadows and smiled. "It's just an old coal room."

She glanced around the dimly lit room. The musty scent

of damp earth filled the air. An old-fashioned washing machine and a rusty bicycle stood beside the stairs. Bare planks lined the walls, serving as shelves. Several boxes and empty jars for home canning rested on the shelves, filled with cobwebs and dead bugs. "You know, this might make a great darkroom for developing my photographs."

"*Darkroom* is right." He squinted, trying to see into each gloomy corner. "You'd need a space heater if you work down here, and some lamps so you can see what you're doing. I have a couple long extension cords you can borrow so you can run some electricity."

"Thank you. That would be great." Her eyes lit up with excitement. "Yes, I think I could fix something up down here."

The sight of her stole his breath. He liked the way her eyes sparkled when she smiled. Nothing contrived. The complete opposite of Cherise Melahn and her simpering smiles. Sam couldn't help contrasting the two women. Rachel seemed so real, so pure.

Gone was the timid, frightened woman. When Lucille Garvey brought her injured dog in to the clinic, Sam had expected Rachel to fly into hysterics. Instead, she'd kept her composure and handled the situation with compassion and professionalism. In the face of Lucille's anguish, Rachel had pushed aside her own fears.

"Thanks for your help at the clinic. I don't know how we would have taken care of Morty without you there to man the front desk." Now he thought about it, he wondered how he ever got along without Rachel there to take charge and keep things running smoothly.

She smiled, looking pleased by his praise. "You're welcome. I just wish I could have done more. Poor Lucille was beside herself with worry."

"Yeah. She's all alone and that dog means an awful lot to

her." In spite of all his animals, he thought of how lonely he felt out at his place. No wife or children to dote upon. No one to share his dreams with. The thought of spending the rest of his life like that left him hollow, empty.

She touched his hand, sending shockwaves of emotion to pierce his heart. "Let's go upstairs. I think our work is finished here."

Our work! It made them seem more and more like a family, and he had no right to insinuate himself into this woman's life. Not after what he'd done to Melanie.

She turned and he followed her upstairs, wishing things could be different between them. Longing to be the kind of man Rachel Walker needed and deserved. But he couldn't change the past, and he only tortured himself by hoping for a future with this or any woman.

As they stepped into the hallway, the bright kitchen light caused him to blink. He clenched and unclenched his fists, wishing things could be different. He'd helped Rachel get set up here at her house and given her a job at his clinic, but he was *not* going to give her any other part of his life or his heart. Period.

The front door slammed. "Mom! Mom, where are you?"

"I'm back here," she called.

Danny rushed into the kitchen, his cheeks red, his snow boots tracking slush across the floor.

As he jerked the knit cap from his head, a thatch of blond hair fell over Danny's brow. "Come quick, Mom. Hurry!"

"What's the matter?" Rachel called, as he headed for the front door and dashed outside. "Danny, it's late and dark out. Come back inside."

"Come see what I found. We have to help them." Danny called over his shoulder as he sprinted across the yard toward Grandpa's old toolshed. The light in the shed had been turned on, its pale glow looking eerie in the darkness.

"Them?" Sam looked at Rachel, and she thought his confused expression mirrored her own.

"I hope it's not a skunk." Her imagination ran wild. The last time she went inside the toolshed, a garter snake nearly scared her to death.

They sprinted across the gravel driveway to the shed. The boy moved too fast and slipped inside before they could catch him. Although the solid structure was almost the size of a two-car garage, Grandpa always called it the toolshed. Sam blocked her path with his wide shoulders. "Let me go first, just to check it out."

Right now, Rachel cared only about protecting her son. Sam didn't allow any opportunity for argument as he pulled one door wide and went inside. Rachel followed on his heels, blinking to give her eyes time to adjust to the lighted interior.

Peg-Boards filled with an assortment of screwdrivers, hammers and other tools lined the walls, just as tidy as the day Grampy died. A layer of dust covered the workbench where Grammy's old toaster still sat, waiting for repairs. Grandpa never got the chance to work on it before the heart attack took him away.

The single bulb overhead splashed hazy light against the rough wooden walls. As a child, Rachel had loved the shed, as long as Grandpa was there with her. She sat for hours on a tall stool, watching him work on one project or another. Back then, she had dreaded the day when summer ended and she must return home. She shuddered to contemplate what kind of person she might have become if not for the influence of her kindly grandparents.

"Danny, what are you doing out here so late at night?"

"I needed a screwdriver."

"What for?"

"To pry open the trunk of one of my toy cars."

"Why?"

"Because I wanted to see what was inside."

She shook her head in frustration. While she'd been mooning over Sam, her son had been cavorting outside in the dark and cold. She needed to concentrate on her boy, not the handsome doctor.

When Danny got down on the floor and climbed back into a dark corner of the shed, a blaze of terror shot up from her toes. "Danny, come out of there right now."

"It's safe, Mom. Come on!" He beckoned to her and she had no choice but to crouch down. They crowded close and Rachel felt Sam's arm brush against hers.

She froze. A gray, mangy cat greeted them, ears laid back, growling and spitting. An old laundry basket filled with rags sat in one snug corner of the shed. Rachel remembered putting the basket there years earlier, to use as a bed for one of her dolls. Now, a baby kitten lay within the folds of rags, mewling and wriggling as it searched for its mother's warm body.

The mother cat hissed.

"Well, I'll be," Sam exclaimed. Slowly, he sat on the floor, watching the cat.

Rachel would have gone right back out the door if his long legs weren't dangling across the floor, blocking her path.

She swallowed hard, her heart racing. "That cat is feral, Danny. She's wild."

The mother cat growled low in the back of her throat, her hair bristling.

"Yes, she's wild. And I'll bet she's hungry." Sam inched his hand into his coat pocket and pulled out a baggie with several strips of bacon inside. "I was saving this treat for Shadow, but I think this cat can use it more."

He spoke to the mother cat, his voice soft and calming as

he tossed a piece of meat to land just in front of her. The cat gave an irritated yowl, sniffed the air, then snatched up the bacon with ferocity. As she tore into the bacon, she remained wary, her glowing eyes never leaving them.

As Sam tossed another piece of meat to the cat, Rachel really looked at the feline for the first time, noticing its thin body and matted fur. With so much snow on the ground, she doubted the animal was catching many mice. A feeling of sympathy crowded Rachel's heart. "What can we do?"

"Feed her."

"Do you have any cat food in your truck?" Rachel's voice squeaked. She could barely take care of herself and Danny. Remembering the goldfish, she didn't want responsibility for any pets. But it would be uncharitable of her to turn her back on the cats. The Savior had compassion for all creatures, great and small.

Sam handed Danny his flashlight. "Danny, go get one of those samples of cat food out of my truck. You know where I keep them."

The boy brushed past, racing for the door.

Sam stretched out, his long body looking completely at home as he sprawled on the rough wood floor. "Her litter was born too late in the season. Once we feed her, she'll have enough milk to take care of her baby."

"Don't cats usually have litters? Where are the rest of her babies?"

"Probably died." He reached for another piece of bacon. "Here, pretty girl. You don't need to fear us. Come on, now, I know you want it."

Pretty girl? This was the ugliest cat Rachel had ever seen. Yet Sam didn't seem to notice. His compassion touched her heart. She supposed the world needed kindhearted veterinarians like him.

Danny returned with a can of cat food. Sam popped the lid and slid it toward the mother. The cat sniffed the air, but wouldn't come that close to the humans.

Danny gave a small croon of sadness. "Ah, Mom, they're all alone. Just like us."

His words bludgeoned Rachel's heart. How could she turn her back on these two pathetic creatures when their lives depended on them? Danny would never forgive her if she didn't do something to help.

Sam glanced at Danny. "We mustn't touch the kitten until it's older or the mother will take it out into the cold to hide it from us. Then it would die. Do you understand? In a couple more weeks, the baby will be able to eat on its own."

Danny nodded solemnly, his bottom lip quivering. "I won't touch it. I don't want the kitten to die."

"Good. I think it's time for us to leave," Sam said.

"But we can't just leave them here. They'll die," Danny argued.

"They should be okay. They're out of the wind and it's warm and dry here. You can bring them more food tomorrow."

Rachel's mouth dropped open. "Wait a minute! I...I can't have an angry cat and her kitten living in my shed."

"Why not?" Sam looked genuinely surprised.

"I don't know how to take care of them." Okay, it was a lame excuse, but all she could come up with at the moment. She wasn't about to explain about the goldfish again.

"Don't worry. I'll help you," he promised. "They'll pretty much take care of themselves. In a couple of weeks, you can take the baby into the house and domesticate it. But the mother's too wild."

Take the kitten into her house? Feeling skeptical, she stared at the mother cat. Its sharp, yellowed teeth and glowing eyes showed no signs of cuddliness. The feline looked fierce and frightened. Wanting to be left alone, yet desperately in need of help.

Just like her and Danny.

"You'll need cats living out here, Rachel," Sam warned, as they went outside and secured the door against the sharp wind. "They'll keep your mice problem under control. Without mousers, you'll be overrun by rodents."

Rachel knew what it was like to be forced to leave her home. How could she chase these poor animals away? And what if this was Grammy's cat, gone wild since Grammy died?

"You can't get rid of them, Mom," Danny exclaimed, his little hands planted on his hips as his eyes welled with tears. "They belong with us. Where would they go? They don't have a daddy to take care of them."

Sam reached out and squeezed Danny's arm. "I'll tell you what. Let's leave the cats alone for now. Later on, we can decide what to do about them, okay?"

Danny's bottom lip jutted out. Rachel would not be able to send the cats away without facing open rebellion from her son. Like it or not, she now had two cats living in her shed.

"Don't worry," Sam reassured the boy. "Now we're here, they've got a good chance at survival."

"You promise?" Danny said.

"I promise we'll do everything we can for them."

The boy threw his arms around Sam in a giant hug and Rachel's throat closed. Her gaze locked with Sam's and she saw hesitancy in his eyes. Slowly, he raised his arms to hug the boy. She couldn't believe how much she had already come to rely on Sam. If their situation continued at this rate, how on earth would she ever be able to keep her distance from the handsome veterinarian?

As they walked back to the house, Danny whispered to Sam. "I knew she'd let me keep them. Moms have soft hearts."

"Yeah, moms are nice that way."

Rachel bit back a laugh. Wait until she told Gladys about this. No doubt they'd share a good chuckle. And then she realized what had been missing from her life during the past year.

Laughter.

Sam coughed, as if to hide his amusement, but then his eyes clouded over and he looked away. In that moment, something changed between them, though she couldn't quite put her finger on what or how. Besides lending her his truck and giving her a job, he'd earned her son's trust. Considering how Danny idolized his father, this was a big step.

Chapter Ten

Wednesday evening after work, Rachel and Danny pulled into the parking lot at the old town hall on Main Street. Built in 1923, the stone structure stood tall and severe beside the modern bank built eight years earlier.

When she shut off the motor, Danny bailed out of the truck and raced over to a group of children from church. Their mothers stood on the sidewalk close by, bundled in coats as they chatted together.

"Hi, there!" Rachel greeted Susan Carter, Martha Keller and Cherise, the waitress from the diner.

"Hello, Rachel. We're just waiting for Gladys. She has the key to let us inside the hall," Martha explained.

"Have you met Cherise Melahn?" Susan indicated the other woman dressed in skintight blue jeans and a short black leather jacket with white fur fringing the collar. Her long blond hair hung across her face, and her wide, brown eyes were ridged with heavy eyeliner.

"Hello, again." Rachel smiled at the other woman.

Cherise gave her a half-smile, her gaze scouring over Rachel. "You're living out at the old Duarte place, right?"

"Yes, they were my grandparents."

Cherise grimaced with disgust. "You couldn't pay me to live in that old house."

Rachel stiffened and bit her tongue. She didn't want to cause a scene by biting back at Cherise's rude comment.

At that moment, Sam pulled up with Gladys and Charlie. As he sat in the truck, his gaze settled on Rachel and he waved.

Gladys puffed over to them. "Sorry I'm late."

"Hi, Sam," Cherise trilled, waving with enthusiasm.

He didn't seem to hear her as he put the truck in gear and pulled away.

Cherise looked disappointed.

"Forget it, Cherise. You're not his type," Susan said.

A sneer curved Cherise's thin lips. "Yes I am. I'm single, aren't I?"

Rachel couldn't explain the blaze of jealousy she felt at that moment. It wasn't her business who Sam dated.

Susan shook her head. "Since you divorced your third husband last month, I suppose so."

"Sam's not your type," Gladys chimed in, as she searched her purse for the keys.

"Yes, he is. He's rich." Cherise laughed, as if she'd said something amusing.

Gladys snorted. "I don't think any man's rich enough for you, girl."

"Well, what is *his* type, then?" Cherise complained.

The other women turned simultaneously and looked at Rachel. Her eyes widened and she held out her hands as if to ward them off. "Wait a minute. Don't bring me into this conversation. I'm not looking."

"But he is." Gladys laughed with delight as she inserted the key in the tall, wooden door.

"Come on, honey. Let's go inside. I want to tell you a few

things about Sam Thorne." Susan linked arms with Rachel as she escorted her inside the hall.

"Like what?"

"Well, I know he likes pumpkin pie. You can cook, can't you?"

Rachel laughed. "Are you suggesting I bake him a pie?"

Susan shrugged. "It couldn't do any harm. He is the most eligible bachelor in Finley. And it doesn't hurt that he's also extremely handsome."

As they stepped into the dark gymnasium, Gladys turned on the lights. Susan pulled away, wearing a satisfied grin while Martha and Gladys shared a conspiratorial smile.

Over the next hour, Rachel frequently caught Cherise glaring at her. Whenever Rachel turned her head, the other woman looked away, giving her the cold shoulder. Without intending to, it seemed Rachel had become the other woman's rival.

As they discussed plans for the annual bazaar fund-raiser, Rachel didn't know what to think. Was Sam looking at her? In a romantic sort of way? How absurd!

She had a full and busy life, with little time to entertain thoughts of her handsome boss. He could look all he wanted to, but she wasn't interested.

Yeah, and pigs could fly.

As time passed, Rachel discovered that working at the clinic never got boring. Every day brought something new and exciting. Though she didn't mind it as much, she never quite got used to handling the animals. On Friday morning, Sam informed her that Charlie was home sick with the flu and Gladys wouldn't be in that day. Rachel didn't fully understand the implications.

"I'll need you to assist me with Frank Thompson's old gelding while I float his teeth today."

"Float his teeth?"

"Yeah, the horse has loose cheek teeth that need to be extracted and filed down. It's called floating," Sam told her.

Oh, this didn't sound good. Rachel could just imagine what the process might entail.

Sam gathered up instruments he would need for the procedure, including a special halter, motorized tools, and hand floats to file off the sharp edges on the horse's teeth.

"Uhm, what about the front office?" She stared at the hypodermic needles and sedatives he set on the counter.

"We'll close up for the next two hours. Unless we have an emergency, drop-ins will have to wait until we return."

Okay, not so odd. He never scheduled appointments on Friday mornings so he could perform scheduled surgeries and take care of procedures such as this. But what would she have to do to assist him?

Gathering her courage, she helped him prepare his implements. "Can you tell me what this will entail?"

"You won't need to do much other than hand me some instruments and help hold the horse's mouth open."

She almost groaned out loud. This sounded messy.

"Don't worry. I've got a pair of rubber gloves you can wear." He chuckled.

She rested one hand on her hip. "You think this is funny?"

"Just a bit."

She pursed her lips together and shook her head. "I just hope I don't let you down."

"You haven't yet."

An hour later, she thought he might have to eat his words. When Frank pulled up with the horse trailer, she put the sign on the front window and locked the door. While Frank unloaded the animal, she stood aside and waited. The men secured the horse in the stocks and Frank stayed nearby during the procedure.

After Sam sedated the quarter horse, he asked Rachel to support the calm animal's head while he put on the halter. The halter kept the horse's head up and allowed Sam to work on the mouth. The procedure went along fine until Sam started extracting loose teeth. Between the horse's ugly tongue, the rank smell of abscessed teeth, blood, and slimy saliva, Rachel's stomach churned with nausea. She felt cold and clammy, and she couldn't understand how Sam did this for a living.

Determined not to faint right there in front of Frank Thompson, she bit her bottom lip and held out to the very end.

"You look kind of pale, ma'am. You okay?" Frank asked, gazing at her face.

She wanted to cry. "Sure, I'm fine."

"Okay, all done." Sam glanced at her. "You don't look so good. Why don't you take a breather while I remove the halter?"

With a quick nod, she stumbled up front to the restroom. She splashed cold water on her face and breathed deeply, settling her nerves. When she joined Sam ten minutes later, she found him explaining to Frank how to administer the antibiotics and the proper dosage.

Without a word, she went up front and sat down, leaning her head against the wall. When the sedative wore off, Frank loaded up his horse and she heard him pull away from the clinic. Minutes later, Sam came up front and squeezed her arm. "Thanks for your help, Rachel. I appreciate you being here."

She lifted her head and looked at him, amazed by his praise. "I almost passed out," she confessed.

"But you didn't. You hung in there. I knew I could count on you."

And then she realized what he said was true. She'd done what he needed. He'd depended on her and she didn't let him down. Though she hadn't liked the job, she felt a sense of accomplishment. A sense of exhilaration and triumph. When she first came to Finley, she never would have believed she could work in a veterinarian clinic. Now, she couldn't imagine doing anything else.

Three days later, Rachel finished the dishes after supper and reached into the top of the coat closet for a pair of gloves. As she thrust her hand inside one glove, her fingers met scratchy paper. Pulling the wad out of the glove, she discovered two twenty-dollar bills folded neatly together. Shaking her head, she chuckled and wondered where else Grammy might have stashed her money.

"Come on, Danny. Get your coat on," she called.

She drove them over to Sam's place to pick up a case of high-calorie cat food. Living on a strict budget, she was grateful for the free samples he offered so she could feed her new pets.

He met them in the front yard, having just come in from one of the corrals. After Sam had put in a full day at the clinic, she thought he worked too hard.

"Hi, Sam!" Danny hollered as he took off at a run toward the red barn. Surrounded by the garage and wide fields of snow, the building dominated the place, sitting off to the side of the house.

"Don't go far. We're not staying long," she called after her son.

"I've never given you a tour of the place." Sam indicated the barn.

"It's getting late. I should be heading home."

"The cat food is inside. It won't take but a few minutes. Come on."

She couldn't resist as he led the way through the wide double doors. Inside, he flipped a switch on the wall. Light flooded the interior, and Rachel gazed up at the high, timbered ceiling. The sweet smell of hay and leather filled the air. Saddles, tack, tools and pitchforks rested on hooks and racks set along one wall. Wheelbarrows, shovels and a small tractor sat beside the door. A tidy row of animal stalls lined the other side.

"Over here. I want to show you something I think you'll like." Sam gestured to one stall in a warm corner of the barn.

Caught up in his excitement, she followed close on his heels.

"Whoa! It looks like someone beat us here." Sam skidded to a halt in front of the low gate of the last stall. He chuckled as he lifted the rope latch on the gate and stepped inside.

"Hi, Mom!" Still wearing his coat and knit cap, Danny sat curled in the straw with three squirming furballs. The puppies squeaked and grunted, scrambling over his legs. The mother dog lay with her head down, calmly watching her babies.

So, this was where Danny disappeared to every time they came to Sam's place.

"Look, Mommy. This one's Pepper, this is Bubbles, and this is Blackie. She's my favorite." As he named the three puppies, he held each one up for her inspection. The pups jumped into his lap, licking his face. The boy giggled and rolled in the hay with his new playmates.

Wary of the mother dog, Rachel took a deep breath and knelt beside her son. Blackie padded across the hay and licked her fingers. Rachel jerked her hand away, but the pup followed until she reached out to feel the dog's downy softness.

"Hey! She likes you, Mom. Sam says dogs choose us, we don't choose them." Her son's face beamed with absolute joy. She had Dr. Thorne to thank for this simple pleasure.

Rachel was startled when the mother rested her head on her thigh. The animal's dark eyes showed no animosity as her eyelids slid closed. Now, what?

"Tabitha likes you," Sam observed.

Hearing her name, the dog opened her eyes just a bit.

"Black Labs are highly intelligent and affectionate." He

reached out and patted the mother's head before scratching her ear. The dog grunted in contentment.

"Sam says he's looking for good homes for the puppies." Danny's eyebrows lifted high, his eyes filled with hope. "Since we're gonna be living out here in the wilds, we might need some protection. Can we keep Blackie, Mom? Can we?"

The wilds? Grammy's house sat five miles outside of town.

"They'll be ready to leave their mother in another week, and you can have your pick of the litter," Sam offered.

Rachel gave a sharp exhale. Danny had been asking for a dog since Alex died. It was normal for little boys to want any and all dogs, bugs and reptiles, but she always said no.

Puppies were definitely preferable to snakes. Even she had to admit Blackie was cute and cuddly. But Rachel now had responsibility for two mangy cats. Surely that was enough. But it was getting harder to put Danny off. Eventually she would have to either get him a dog or tell him absolutely not and then deal with his sadness. Right now, she hated causing him more pain. Which meant they would get a dog.

Eventually.

She looked up at Sam, who watched the boy with delight. He glanced at her, then coughed, as if to stifle a laugh.

She moved closer to her son. "Danny, I think we need to get more settled before we take on any more responsibility, don't you agree?"

"Ah," he groaned. "I can take care of Blackie. She only eats a little. And I'll clean up her messes, Mom."

His begging made her feel small for denying him, but she just couldn't agree. Not right now.

"We'll see. You heard Sam. They're not old enough to leave their mother yet." She stood and backed out of the stall, hoping Danny didn't persist. Frankly, she wasn't up to a disagreement with him right now.

An expression of panic crossed Danny's face. "Don't make me go yet, Mom. Can't I stay just a few more minutes, please?"

She smiled and nodded, without the heart to rip him away from such bliss. "Sure. We'll leave in just a bit."

Sam followed Rachel outside the gate, closing it behind him. "What about finishing our tour?"

"Yes, please." Anything to leave the barn.

He smiled and headed outside where he led her toward another, smaller building. Opening the double bifold doors, he waited for her to enter before him. She paused at the threshold, peering inside.

"This is my workshop." He flipped on the light, revealing maple cabinets, shelves, benches, Peg-Boards filled with tools, and a large work area. Sitting to one side was a small, half-finished oak table. A sander and discs rested beside the elegantly carved legs. Though the wood looked freshly sanded, no evidence of sawdust remained. Sam must have cleaned up after his work.

She gravitated toward the table, resting her fingertips on the silky-smooth top. "Did you make this?"

"Yeah. It's a work in progress." He chuckled, his complexion turning red.

My, oh, my! Dr. Sam Thorne had a grain of shyness in him. Surprising for such a confident, self-assured man. Somehow, his discomfiture made him seem more vulnerable.

"It's beautiful," she said.

"Thank you." He showed a half-smile. "I'm making it for Gladys, so I'd appreciate it if you didn't tell her."

"I won't say a word." She enjoyed their little secret. It felt good to be included, but she couldn't explain why.

He changed the subject. "Some day, I'd like to build a surgical center here, complete with a lab and an MRI machine."

As she watched him talk about his plans, she felt odd.

Except for Alex, no one ever confided their dreams to her. This moment seemed a bit too personal. She couldn't help agreeing with Cherise's observation. Sam had everything.

He was the kind of man a woman could fall in love with.

He looked at her and her face flushed with heat. "Is there some problem?"

A shake of her head was all she could manage. She'd come to Finley to make a fresh start for her and Danny, not to become entangled with a magnetic man.

"It's getting late and I should get Danny home." Her voice didn't tremble too much.

She waited by the clunker while Sam went to fetch Danny. Laughter caught her attention and she turned to see her son chasing after the doctor, Sam's big black dog, Shadow, romping at their feet.

Sam hoisted Danny up on his shoulders, then raced across the yard, his deep laughter mingling with the little boy's. The dog barked, its tongue lolling over ridges of sharp teeth. Rachel prepared herself to jerk open the door and jump inside the truck, but the dog didn't come near her.

Danny opened up his arms like an airplane, his face alight with joy. When he saw her, he yelled. "Look, Mom! I'm flying. I'm flying!"

She smiled and waved, almost overcome with emotion at seeing her son so happy. Tears burned her eyes, and she brushed them away before wrapping her arms around herself, feeling a sudden chill that had nothing to do with the weather. That old feeling of vulnerability engulfed her, filled with nostalgia and regret.

If only Sam were Alex.

Chapter Eleven

The following Saturday morning, Rachel bundled Danny in two sweatshirts, snow boots, his warmest winter coat, hat and gloves. Along with a pot of homemade chili, she packed extra clothing in case he got wet and cold from the snow.

She chuckled as he trundled out to the truck in a stiff shuffle, hardly able to move. When they pulled into the church parking lot, Rachel saw numerous people milling about. Dressed to play in the snow, the adults laughed and talked in huddles while the kids ran around throwing snow at each other in the field nearby.

Several trucks with snowmobiles in the back sat parked at the side of the road. As she got out of Sam's clunker, Rachel saw Susan Carter standing on the curb.

"Stop playing so rough. Someone's gonna get hurt," Susan warned her children as they wrestled in the snow.

The kids ignored her, their screams and laughter filling the air as they continued their play.

"Hi, Susan," Rachel called, as she zipped up her coat and walked over to join her.

Susan shifted the toddler she held on her hip, the child

wrapped up like a little Eskimo. "Hi. Are you going on this expedition?"

Rachel took a deep breath and let it go. "Yes, I'm afraid so. How about you?"

"Not on your life." Susan chuckled. "Tom's gonna take our three oldest kids and leave me here to get some laundry done. Believe it or not, that sounds like a holiday for me."

Since Susan had four children, Rachel assumed any time Susan had to herself must feel like a vacation, even if she did have to keep working. "I don't know how you have time to serve on the committee for the bazaar fund-raiser."

Susan adjusted the ties on her baby's hat. "It's easy. Martha's the chairwoman and does most of the organization. She calls and bounces ideas off me, and I just go along for the ride. I work on projects all year long, and toss cookies and loaves of bread in the freezer so when the day arrives I'm all ready. No big deal."

"You're being modest. I know you do a lot more than that."

"Mommy!" A child's wail broke into their conversation. Susan's five-year old son ran toward them, a trickle of blood dripping from his nose. As predicted, the children's play had become too rough.

"Oh, no!" Susan heaved a big sigh. "I better go. See you next week at the committee meeting."

Rachel waved, her gaze scanning the crowd of children for Danny. He stood out in the field, helping Charlie and some other boys his age build an igloo in the deep snow. He waved, and his happy exuberance filled her with delight. Maybe this outing was just what they both needed.

Rachel turned and saw Sam leaning against his truck, his arms crossed. Her pulse quickened at the sight of him. Shorty Keller, Fred Baxter and Vic Lockhart stood beside him. At that moment, he threw his head back and laughed at something Vic said. Dressed in tan coveralls, he had the top portion unzipped and lowered off his shoulders, dangling loose around his waist. Wearing a white, long-sleeved sweatshirt underneath, he appeared completely comfortable without a coat. She wondered how he could stand the cold. Maybe the heavy coveralls, blue knit ski cap, and snow boots gave him enough warmth.

He looked up, his eyes locking with hers. She turned away, embarrassed to be caught staring. Out of the corner of her eye, she saw him sauntering toward her. To cover up her nervousness, she made a pretense of adjusting the scarf around her neck.

"Hi, there!" Sam's quirky smile creased the dimple in his left cheek.

"Hello." She smiled back. She couldn't help herself.

His gaze swept her. When he reached up and brushed a strand of hair away from her cheek, she felt giddy as a young girl. "You ready to go snowmobiling?"

She shook her head. "I'm going along, but I thought I'd stay in Fred's cabin and help the other women prepare lunch instead of snowmobiling."

"Ah, you have to go at least once, just so you can say you've tried it. The other women find time to take a ride, too. There's nothing like it. The breeze whipping past as you speed across the snow. It's great."

Listening to his animated description, she found herself longing to try it. "Okay, maybe once."

He smiled and nodded toward his truck. "Why don't you leave the clunker here at the church? You and Danny can climb in with Charlie and me. No sense in taking two vehicles up on the mountain. I'll bring you back here after the activity is over."

"Gladys isn't here?"

"Nope. She's not big on snowmobiling. She asked me to take Charlie while she stays home and gets some chores done."

Smart lady. Truthfully, Rachel didn't know what she

thought of this snowmobiling thing. She couldn't help wishing she had a husband to take Danny while she stayed behind and got some work done at home. She was a bit uncertain about driving up to the mayor's cabin on Thimble Mountain, where she might get stuck. Though she'd never been there before, she understood from the announcements in church that while it was a beautiful winter paradise, the snow was deep and treacherous. Knowing Sam and many other families from her congregation would be there gave her a sense of confidence. She felt like she belonged here with them.

"Okay," she heard herself answer.

"Let's go! Daylight's a'burning!" Bill Sawyer shouted, waving his arms to get everyone's attention.

"Come on, boys," Sam called to Danny and Charlie.

The children came running, breathless and excited, their faces red and smiling.

The ride took forty minutes. A procession of trucks followed in tandem along the narrow dirt road circling Thimble Mountain, driving slow in 4-wheel drive. As they thumped along the rough terrain, Rachel gave thanks she'd had the wisdom to climb in with Sam instead of negotiating this road on her own.

When they arrived at Fred Baxter's cabin, they parked along the side of the road and clambered out of the truck. Children's laughter and adult voices echoed in the clear, mountain air, their breaths exhaling in little puffs of smoke. Although cold, the sun glimmered off the snow, and its brightness prompted Rachel to put on her sunglasses and earmuffs.

Sam zipped up his coveralls and tugged on his heavy leather gloves. Then, he climbed into the back of his truck, moving with confident ease. She admired his masculine strength as he lowered a long ramp past the tailgate. When he jerked back the blue tarp, his black snowmobile gleamed in the sunlight, sporting a single white stripe down each side. He turned on the machine and backed it out onto the snow-packed ground.

"Yippee! Come on!" Charlie yelled.

The two boys raced to the truck where Charlie retrieved two helmets. One large enough for an adult, the other one small enough for a child or a woman.

Rachel joined them, watching as Sam put on his helmet.

"Who wants to go first?" He looked at Rachel, his dark eyes crinkled with merriment.

"Are you sure this is safe?" She couldn't hide a hint of concern.

He smiled, showing that endearing dimple. "It's only as dangerous as the driver, and I can assure you I'm very safe."

Having watched him romp and play with the boys, she had some doubts. He was the type of rough-and-tumble man who loved sports and good food. But she'd also seen his gentle side. He seemed to know when to play and when to be serious.

Charlie gave Danny a gentle shove toward the snowmobile. "Since it's your first time, why don't you go first?"

"Thanks!" Delighted by the invitation, Danny pulled on the helmet and Rachel helped buckle the strap beneath his chin.

Sam straddled the snowmobile, his long legs stretched forward as he rested his booted heels against the foot ramps. He turned the key and started the engine while Danny climbed on behind.

"Wrap your arms around my waist and hold on tight. If you need to stop, just tug sharply on my side like this." Sam showed Danny how to grab folds of his coveralls and pull hard. "Got it?"

"Got it." Danny nodded, taking all of this very seriously.

"Okay, let's go!" Sam winked at Rachel. "We'll be back soon."

With a roar, the snowmobile surged away, whipping over the snow with ease. Other snowmobiles joined them, the roar deafening as they bounced over hills, zipping up inclines and skirting around large trees. Rachel hoped someone didn't mistake a snow-covered boulder for a soft hillside.

To take her mind off her worries, she turned to face Charlie. There must be something she could do with the little boy while he awaited his turn to ride.

"Want to build a snowman?" Charlie suggested.

What a great idea! "Sure!"

He scooped up a handful of snow and packed it into a hard ball. He rolled it through the snow to add to its bulk and create the base for the snowman. She did likewise, building the middle section. By that time, several other children came to join in the fun. They worked for some time, laughing at the uneven shape of the bloated bottom. They had just finished the third and final tier when Sam and Danny returned.

"Mom! It was great. You're gonna love it," Danny said, as he scrambled off the snowmobile and stumbled toward her. She could barely make out his eyes through the droplets of melted snow on his face guard.

"You want to go next? Climb aboard," Sam drawled.

Danny removed his helmet and handed it to her. She held it by the chinstrap, staring at it as if a dead rat dangled from her fingers.

"Don't worry. The kids can finish Mr. Nichols while we're gone." He inclined his head toward the snowman.

"Mr. Nichols?"

"My old science teacher from high school. Your snowman reminds me of him."

The children laughed. They still hadn't added eyes or a nose to the snowman.

"Mr. Nichols didn't have a face?"

Sam nodded. "Yeah, he had a scrunched face and a lumpy bottom."

She giggled. This man made her feel young and free, so refreshing after all the sadness she'd endured. She glanced at the cabin, where numerous adults sat on lawn chairs on the porch, sipping cups of hot chocolate. Placing one hand on her waist, she considered the snowman for several moments before glancing at the children. "You kids think you can do something to make Mr. Nichols look a little better before I return from my ride?"

"Sure!" Danny scrubbed at the uneven bulges on the base of the snowman with his gloved hands. She could see the tip of his tongue pressed against his top lip as he concentrated on his work.

Laughing at his serious expression, Rachel turned to look at Sam. His long body draped the snowmobile, all legs, chest and arms. He leaned one elbow against the steering bars, watching her with a lopsided grin.

As she walked toward him, a feeling of uncertainty replaced the laughter in her heart. The thought of riding about the mountainside with her arms wrapped around this man's waist gave her a feeling of unease. She hadn't hugged another man since Alex died.

She backed up a step. "Maybe Charlie would like to go next."

"I think he's occupied." Sam pointed at the children, who were completely engrossed in finding rocks they could use for a mouth and eyes. "Come on. We won't be gone long."

How could she resist? Though nervous, she wanted to go. Besides, he'd think her a sissy if she refused.

Her body trembled as she climbed onto the machine. She gripped the vinyl strap in front of her as if she prepared to ride a wild bronco.

"You ready?" he asked over his shoulder, a hint of laughter in his voice.

"You're enjoying this too much," she scolded.

"And you're not enjoying it enough." He revved the motor. "It might be better if you hold on to me."

Not if she could help it.

The snowmobile surged forward. The first bump caused her to grab on to his waist in automatic reflex. He folded one hand over hers, patting her twice. That simple gesture broke through her defenses like nothing else could. His touch brought her comfort, lifting her spirits. In his presence, she could almost forget her troubles.

As Sam gathered speed on the snowmobile, she gripped the folds of his coveralls. Faster and faster they went, bouncing over drifts of snow. Shards of snow dust spiked the sharp wind and lashed against her like a whip. Thank goodness for the face guard, which protected her from windburn.

She tucked her face against his shoulder, peeking out as other snowmobilers whizzed past. Bill Sawyer and his wife, Becky, waved at them, but Rachel didn't dare let go of Sam long enough to return the gesture. After several minutes of driving through the forest, they emerged along a snowy plateau. Sam slowed the machine and pulled to a stop, letting the motor idle.

"Look at that." He pointed toward the western mountains, where snow-laden pine trees dotted the skyline. A deer leapt across the clearing and disappeared into the sheltering trees. Rachel stared in awe as the sun glinted off the snowcapped peaks.

"Beautiful!" she breathed. "Isn't it amazing how the Lord provides for us? He never ceases to amaze me."

Sam glanced at her face but didn't say anything. She studied his thoughtful expression and furrowed brow. "Is something bothering you, Sam?"

Now what made her ask that? he wondered.

"Nope." He didn't look at her. "You're entitled to your feelings, but God hasn't been too kind to me in the past."

"How so?" She knew it would serve her right if he told her to mind her own business.

"I'd rather not talk about it."

His rigid shoulders told her to drop the subject, yet a sudden urge to comfort him forced her to speak what was in her heart. "I didn't mean to pry. But I can tell you the Lord gives us trials to help strengthen our faith. We just have to trust in Him."

He snorted and kneaded his right shoulder, as if to ease a tightness in the muscle. "God can give me all the trials He wants, but I don't cotton to Him messing with the lives of people I love."

Yes, definitely harboring angst over some past tragedy. "Are you talking about Melanie?"

"How do you know about her?"

"I pay attention."

In his eyes, she saw raw pain. "Yes, Melanie."

"What happened to her, Sam?"

He hesitated and she thought he might avoid her question. "Twelve years ago, she died in my arms. I…I was driving the car that night. It was late and I lost control. She wasn't wearing her seat belt. I suffered a broken wrist and a concussion while she lost her life."

His candor surprised her. Somehow she knew the admission didn't come easy for him and she felt humbled that he would confide in her. "And you blame yourself?"

"Of course I do." He met her gaze and she saw scalding grief written on his face.

"I'm sorry, Sam. I understand you must be torn up over what happened, but it was an accident. You shouldn't keep torturing yourself over it."

His face contorted with anguish. "I wish it were that simple, Rachel."

"What do you mean?"

He locked his jaw and she realized he wasn't telling her everything. She longed to ask him for more information, but knew she'd pressed him far enough. Still, she couldn't help wondering what really happened the night Melanie died.

"We better get back." He revved the motor and she gripped folds of his coveralls.

The return ride took longer. Sam drove at an even pace, seeming more subdued. Rachel would die before admitting she felt the same. Out here, she could lose herself in the beauty of the day and almost forget her fears and concerns. But they had to return to reality.

Back at the cabin, Rachel climbed off the snowmobile as Charlie came running to take his turn. She helped him buckle the helmet beneath his chin, then stepped back and waved as he and Sam zipped away.

Danny stood beside her, wrapping one arm around her waist as he waved goodbye. He breathed a deep sigh of contentment, his little chest expanding. "Mom, this is the best day ever."

She hugged him tight, almost agreeing, but she remembered a couple of other days that topped this one: her marriage and the day she gave birth to Danny.

They worked on the snowman for a time, then Rachel left Danny with the other children while she went inside the cabin to help prepare lunch.

The women carried baskets of food inside while several men set up long tables on the front porch of the spacious cabin. Rachel helped the other women make ham-and-turkey sandwiches and hot chili. When everything was ready, she carried platters of food outside to set up buffet style.

"Come and eat," Bill Sawyer called, and the children came running.

As she carried a heavy bowl of potato chips in one arm and a package of foam cups in the other, Rachel tripped and almost did a head dive off the porch. Sam appeared out of nowhere, catching her just in time.

"Let me help you." His smile and dark eyes filled her view as he took the bowl and cups.

"Thank you. It seems you're always saving me from catastrophe."

His warm breath grazed her cheek. "It's my pleasure."

"Okay, everyone. Let's gather around and I'll say a blessing on the food." Bill folded his arms, waiting for everyone to become reverent before he offered a prayer.

Afterward, they sat on fallen tree trunks, holding their plates in their laps while they took pleasure in the simple meal and happy conversation. Rachel thoroughly enjoyed herself.

While she helped clear the tables, Sam took the boys out for another ride. When they prepared to go home, she stood back and watched as Sam drove the snowmobile up the ramp and into the back of his truck. He closed the tailgate and clapped his hands twice. "Okay, let's get rolling."

Rachel and the boys piled into the truck. When Sam climbed into the cab and closed the door, he looked over at her. His smile made her feel all warm and mellow inside.

"Did you have a good time today?" he asked.

"Yes, snowmobiling is definitely a lot of fun." She spoke the truth. She even looked forward to the next time.

By the time they arrived back at the church, darkness had fallen. Sam helped her load Danny into the clunker. The boy curled up in his seat, his eyelids drooping with fatigue.

"Thanks for a lovely day, Sam. I really appreciate all you've done to help Danny and me."

"No problem. You're coming over to help Gladys prepare Sunday dinner tomorrow, aren't you?"

She knew she should stay home and fix dinner at her house, but she said, "Okay."

He smiled and stepped back as she put the truck in gear and pulled away. She watched him for several moments in her rearview mirror. Charlie joined him, and he wrapped an arm around the boy's shoulders. Like Danny, Charlie had no father, but he was lucky enough to have a kind uncle who took an interest in him. Both boys needed a father figure in their lives, to teach them service to others and how to become a good man. Rachel appreciated Sam even more.

Tomorrow, she'd see him again. The thought sent an unexpected thrill up her spine. She tried to tell herself it was nothing. And yet, she knew her feelings for Sam had changed. She'd see him again tomorrow. So, why did she miss him so much right now?

Chapter Twelve

The next afternoon, Rachel stood at the kitchen sink in Sam's kitchen, washing up the last few dishes from Sunday dinner. Although she didn't always accept, Sam and Gladys invited her and Danny over every week.

The TV sounded from the living room, some cartoon left on by the boys. They'd hurriedly pulled on their winter coats and raced out the door with Gladys to drive over to the clinic to check on the animals for the night. Sam had been called out earlier by a rancher with an ailing horse. Being alone in Sam's kitchen brought Rachel peace. She felt completely at home in this house.

A dull thud sounded at the back door. Sam came inside, his nose and cheeks red from the cold. He looked up and smiled as he doffed his coat and hung it on the hook by the door.

"Brrr! I wouldn't be surprised if the temperature dips below zero tonight." He pulled off his gloves and set them by the heat vent on the floor to dry.

"Did you see the boys?" she asked, as she rinsed another plate.

"Nope, but I'm sure they'll be here soon." He stepped over to the utility sink and washed his hands before picking up a towel to help her dry the plates.

For a few minutes, they stood working together in companionable silence. Rachel couldn't explain the domestic feeling that settled over her.

"How's Danny feeling these days?" he asked.

She cleared her voice. "Fine. Why?"

"I thought he might still be upset after mistaking Marvin Sewell for his father."

"I think he realizes his daddy won't be coming back. It's been hard for him to accept."

"I'm sure he misses his father pretty bad." He opened the cupboard and piled a stack of clean plates on the first shelf.

"Yes, we both do."

Silence filled the room, heavy and oppressive.

"It might help if you talk about her." Now, why did she say that? She had no right to encourage Sam to speak about his secret pain.

"Who?"

"Melanie." Her voice sounded small.

He hung the dish towel on the oven door and backed toward the laundry room, where he'd left his coat and gloves. "I can't, Rachel."

"I understand, really I do." She reached out to touch his arm, but he jerked away.

"You understand nothing," he growled.

She flinched at the fury in his voice. Looking at his face, she expected to see anger. Instead, she saw so much misery in his eyes that she wondered how a man could torture himself like this for so long. A part of her envied Melanie. How she wished Alex had loved her this much. Deep down, she knew her husband had loved her in his own way, but never like this. Never so completely.

"Neither she nor the Lord would want you to torture yourself like this, Sam."

"How do you know? You don't know Melanie."

"I do know if she was any kind of woman worth having, she'd hate to see you in this kind of pain."

"You don't understand, Rachel. The Lord will never forgive me for…" His voice trailed off.

"The Lord forgives everyone, Sam. I believe that's what the Atonement was for. The Savior took our sins upon himself. Blaming yourself for Melanie's death won't bring her back. Guilt is only good if it helps us modify our behavior. You can't change the accident that took her life."

He looked at her, his brow crinkled in thought, his big hands clenched by his sides. "I wish it were that simple. But I'm not about to explain it to you."

He shook his head and his breathing came hard and sharp. She thought for just one moment that he might break down and sob. She hated seeing him like this. Hated causing this strong, gentle man any more pain.

She took a step toward him. "Maybe I can help—"

"Don't!" He slashed the air with his hand and she froze. "Don't ask things you're not willing to give in return."

"What do you mean?" she asked, knowing deep down he was right. She shouldn't question him like this, yet something compelled her to continue…as if the words weren't her own and a higher power induced her to push on without heed.

"What about Alex?" His voice held a hint of censure and his sarcasm bordered on cruelty. As if he wanted to hurt her as much as she was hurting him by forcing him to answer her questions. "Don't you think you ought to tell me everything about your own past?"

"Like what? There's nothing to tell."

"What happened to your husband?"

"He died, Sam. He had a brain aneurysm. It wasn't anyone's fault. He just died, and we never got to say goodbye."

Tears sprang to her eyes and poured down her cheeks so fast that she had little chance to gather her strength and stop them.

"And why did you come here to Finley?"

Ah, he had her now. She trusted Sam and he'd proven himself to be a good friend, but once she crossed the line and spoke the truth, she couldn't take it back. It'd be out there for anyone to hear. Out of her control. "Okay…I'm broke. Is that what you wanted to hear? I don't think it takes a rocket scientist to see that my husband left us with nothing. Not even enough life insurance to pay for his funeral. All I have in this world is my son and Grammy's run-down farmhouse. So, I came here to Finley to make a fresh start. If it weren't for you, I wouldn't even have a car or a way to earn a living."

"I'm sorry, Rachel. I never meant to—"

She held up a hand. "No apology needed. I know I've never been completely alone. Even in my darkest hour, the Lord has always been there for me. I don't believe we were put on this earth to have an easy time of it. I believe we were put here to learn and grow and walk by faith. We can't do that sitting cozily in a grand house with lots of money and never any ailments or loss. I've done nothing wrong and neither have you. When we feel sorry for ourselves, it's easy to overlook our blessings. But if you look for God in your life, you'll find Him, Sam."

So, she'd drawn the chalk line. But which of them would cross it first? Without trust, they couldn't move forward in their relationship. How could they ever heal unless they were both willing to speak the truth? To vent their pasts and be willing to let go.

She opened her mouth to tell Sam about her secret yearning to find happiness and love once more. She couldn't do it. Her tongue felt like a chunk of wood inside her mouth. Absolute terror made her freeze where she stood. She stared at him in silence, wishing she didn't feel this way. Wishing her hands didn't tingle every time Sam Thorne walked into the room.

She watched as he grabbed his coat and gloves, ducked his head, turned and opened the door and left. The soft click of the latch closing seemed to reanimate her, and she stepped over to the window. She looked out, watching Sam's tall frame as he sauntered toward the barn.

She didn't blink as he disappeared inside. She sank to her knees right there on the kitchen floor. Throwing her head back, she inhaled deeply, staring at the black-and-white cat clock hanging on the wall. Its mechanical tail swung back and forth, counting off the seconds, as if keeping beat with her heart.

Her breath caught in her throat and a strangled cry rose upward from her chest. Gripping the leg of one kitchen chair, she took several gasping breaths. She felt as though her heart were exploding inside her chest, as though she'd lost Alex all over again. Tears flooded her eyes and she wept.

The next day, Rachel awoke early so she wouldn't be late for work. While she put a load of laundry in the washing machine, Danny hurried out to the tool shed to feed the cats. He returned to the house howling with tears.

"She…she's dead, Mommy. She's dead."

He held the mother cat's stiff corpse. The baby kitten mewled, sticking her head out of his front coat pocket.

Rachel looked at her son's grief-stricken face and her heart wrenched painfully. She never wanted this cat, but it hurt her deeply that she'd died.

Reaching for a paper sack, she held it open for Danny. "Put her in here, son. We'll give her a proper burial later tonight, okay?"

She spoke gently, hoping a funeral would ease his suffering. He'd lost too much over the past year, and she hated for him to lose any more.

He surrendered the mother cat, his shoulders trembling with

sobs. The gray kitten mewled and Danny held the baby, his eyes never leaving the paper sack as Rachel closed it up and set it out on the back porch where wild animals couldn't get it.

Rachel knelt beside him, resting one hand on his shoulder. "What did you decide to name your kitten?"

"St…Stripe," he hiccuped. "Because she has a little white line of fur running down her front leg." He traced his finger over the kitten's paw.

"That's a good name."

"Are you gonna die like Daddy?" His sad eyes lifted and she saw the fear and uncertainty there.

She hugged him, careful not to mash the kitten. "No, son. I'm not going to die for a very long time."

"Why'd the momma cat die?" He sniffed.

"She was old, and I think the winter was just too hard on her. But we still have Stripe. We'll take her to the clinic and Sam will teach us how to care for her."

"But Sam promised me they'd be okay."

"No, he promised we'd take good care of them. And we have."

"But what if Stripe dies, too?"

Why did kids have to ask such difficult questions? "She won't. She's young and strong and there's no reason for her to die anytime soon."

"I don't want Stripe anymore." Jerking away, he thrust the kitten at her, then ran for the front door. Rachel went after him, fearing what he might do. He got into the beat-up truck, looking straight ahead, his little jaw locked, his eyes hard. He'd been like this after Alex died, too. Hurt and remote. Fearing he might lose someone or something else he loved dearly.

Rachel quickly gathered their lunches and her purse, then tucked the kitten inside her coat before she locked the front door and went to join her son. Inside the truck, she let the windows defrost. She tried to speak to Danny, but he brushed her off, silent and angry. If only she could ease his pain. She left him alone, giving him time to cool off.

At the clinic, Sam met her and Danny at the door. Danny glared and brushed past the doctor without saying one word. He joined Charlie out back to help feed and water the animals.

"Is something wrong?" Sam's eyes narrowed with concern.

The kitten's muffled mewling came from inside Rachel's coat and Sam looked curious. Rachel held the bundle of fur out to Sam. "I'm afraid the mother died sometime in the night. I didn't dare leave the baby in the shed for fear she'd freeze to death, so I brought her here."

Sam scooped the kitten into his big hands. "I'm sorry. I take it Danny's pretty upset right now."

Rachel nodded. "What can we do to save the baby?"

"Come with me." Sam took her to the back where he got out a special can of milk and a doll-sized bottle. He showed Rachel how to hold and feed the kitten.

The baby made little sucking sounds as milk bearded the fur around her mouth. Before long, Rachel found herself enjoying the task. "Thank you, Sam."

"You're welcome, Rachel." He watched her with glowing eyes and she looked back at the baby.

Before the boys walked to school, Sam tried to show Danny how to feed Stripe. "She needs us more now than ever, son. We can't turn our backs on her or she'll die. It's not her fault her mother died and we can't be mean to her, can we?"

The boy gazed at Stripe, his eyes filled with bitterness. Then, he faced Sam. "I'm *not* your son."

Rachel gasped. "Danny!"

The boy fled, racing out the back door of the clinic to join Charlie on their walk to school.

"I'm sorry, Sam. He's upset right now."

Sam gave a sad smile. "It's understandable. He's still hurting from losing his father, and now he's lost the mother cat. He feels threatened by me."

"But you haven't done anything to him."

Sam reached out and cupped her cheek with his palm. "Yeah, I've done something Danny's noticed, even if you refuse to see it."

His touch sent shock waves of electricity coursing through her. "And what is that?"

"I've fallen for his mother, and he fears I might try to take his father's place."

She stepped back, her breath whooshing out of her in a quick exhale. Sam turned and walked away, leaving Rachel to mull his words over in her brain. Sam had fallen for her. As in, fallen in love with her?

Oh, her poor, battered son. She couldn't believe his courage in spite of the tragedies he'd been forced to endure at such a young age. How she loved and respected him. And yet, she didn't know how to help him through his grief. Prayer was her only weapon.

Chapter Thirteen

The following days were a whirlwind of activity for Rachel and Danny. When not working at the clinic, she served on the bazaar fund-raiser committee or toiled on their new home, painting, cleaning and wallpapering the dreary walls. Like a little trooper, Danny helped by fetching tools, holding the ladder, sorting boxes and being the man of the house.

The few times they went over to Sam's Place, Danny made a beeline for the barn and she always found him hunkered back in the straw, playing with Blackie. This precipitated a begging spree in which Danny asked when he could take Blackie home. To which Rachel insisted the dog was still too young. To which Sam remained quiet on the subject. It didn't matter. The time was fast approaching when Rachel would have to either relent or tell Danny he could not have the dog. At all.

Whenever she went into town, Rachel took Danny to the general store and let him peruse the toys so she could see what he wanted for his birthday. Nothing caught his eye except dogs. Dogs everywhere. Loping down the street, at the clinic, outside of church. He had to pet every canine they came across.

"Danny, be sure to ask the owner first. Not all dogs are nice, and you don't want to get bit."

"Ah, Mom. They're not gonna bite me." He pulled away from her, a mutinous frown tugging at his forehead.

Please, Father in Heaven, help me reconcile myself to having a dog. Help me not be afraid anymore.

She felt trite bothering God with such a trivial request, but she didn't know where else to turn with her dilemma. Even after working at Sam's clinic all this time, she still disliked touching dogs unless absolutely necessary. In her view, Morty didn't count. He'd been incredibly wounded and needed her help.

Fretting over her dilemma, she set up a darkroom in the basement of her farmhouse and found solace working there on her photography at night after Danny went to bed. They no longer had Sunday dinner over at Sam's house with Gladys and Charlie. She had loved cooking with Gladys in Sam's big kitchen, listening to the boys romping around the house, their squeals of laughter as Sam wrestled with them, but Danny seemed to resent Sam more and more. As if he suspected the man of trying to usurp his father's place in his mother's life.

Instead, after dinner at their own house, Rachel would take a drive through town with her son. While she looked for unique subjects for her camera lens, they would chat and the topic always came around to dogs. No matter how much Rachel tried to tantalize her son with a new red fire engine or a shiny blue bicycle for his birthday, he always shook his head.

"Nope, I don't want a fire engine." He pressed his lips together and looked straight ahead.

Yeah, Rachel knew. If Danny couldn't have his father, then he wanted a dog and nothing else.

The week before Danny's birthday, Rachel carried a heavy cardboard box into the town hall. Filled with four loaves of homemade pumpkin bread and ten framed photographs she had taken around town, she propped the box on her hip.

"Wow!" Danny stood beside her, gazing about the spacious room that served as a gymnasium, recreation and meeting hall. Now, Rachel was glad Gladys had insisted she participate in the bazaar. She'd had fun planning for the event with the rest of the committee members.

Music blared over a karaoke machine set on the stage at the front of the room. The fragrant scent of cinnamon and cloves engulfed her. Bright lights and laughter from the work crew filled the air. As Rachel set her burden on a table by the door, she looked around.

"Hi, Rachel!" Martha Keller waved from the top of a ladder set beneath a basketball hoop at one end of the hall. She twisted a strand of red and green lights around the hoop and backboard. Susan Carter stood on the floor, holding the ladder so it wouldn't wobble.

"Hi there! Where would you like me to put this?" She indicated her box.

Martha climbed down and both women came over to inspect Rachel's offerings.

Susan picked up one loaf of bread and sniffed. "Yum! Smells delicious. How did you get such nice, full loaves?"

Pleased by Susan's kind words, Rachel shrugged. "It's Grammy's old recipe."

Both women gasped.

"Do you know what this means?" Susan asked.

"Once people know, it'll sell quick," Martha said.

"I miss Myra so much. I'd love her recipe," Susan gushed.

"Maybe." Rachel smiled, but had no intention of sharing her grandmother's recipe with anyone. Grammy had won numerous blue ribbons at the county fair with this bread. The day Grammy gave her the recipe, she'd warned Rachel never to reveal the secret formula, not even to Lucille, her best friend. Since Rachel had plans to enter the fair this coming summer, she determined it would not be prudent to divulge Grammy's ingredients.

"If your bread tastes as good as it looks, it's too good for the baked-goods table. We'll put these loaves on the cake auction table. People will pay plenty once they know it's Myra's recipe." Susan picked up two loaves, eyeing them with envy.

"Really?" The pressure was on and Rachel stared at the pretty loaves she'd made, hoping their taste lived up to her grandmother's reputation.

"Absolutely." Susan leaned closer to Martha and a wicked gleam filled her eyes. "Lucille Garvey will be pea-green with envy."

"Why?" Rachel asked in confusion.

Martha showed a smug smile. "Her bread won the county fair this past summer only because your grandmother wasn't there to compete with her. She'll be furious when she finds out you're using Myra's recipe."

Rachel tensed. She knew her grandmother had a friendly rivalry with Lucille, but never thought it might be this serious.

The two women laughed as they carried the loaves away. Rachel stared after them, half-tempted to return her bread to the truck. She didn't want trouble, especially with Lucille. She liked the older woman and didn't want to hurt her feelings.

"Hi, Rachel."

She turned and found Gladys looking over her shoulder at the box of black-and-white photographs she'd carefully wrapped between sheets of newspaper. "Are those for the sale?"

"Yes. Where do you want them?" Rachel fingered the cardboard box, hoping people would buy them.

"How about over here?" Gladys indicated an empty table

already decorated with a green plastic tablecloth and garlands of holly.

"Hey, there's Charlie." Danny pointed to where the other boy stood peering at the tables of baked goods. Danny's eyes widened when he saw the fudge, divinity, peanut brittle and other treats spread out for people to purchase and take home.

"Can I go, Mom? Can I?"

Rachel reached into her purse and took out five one-dollar bills, which she folded and tucked into his hand. "Don't eat so much junk you make yourself sick."

"Thanks, Mom!" Danny hugged her before racing off to join Charlie.

Gladys stood close beside Rachel and chuckled as she watched the two boys greet one another. "Telling a seven-year-old not to eat candy is like throwing kerosene on a fire."

Rachel laughed. "Good thing I fed him a nutritious dinner. I figure he can't do too much damage with the little money I gave him."

"It won't matter. When Sam arrives, he'll give the boys whatever they want." Gladys pursed her lips.

Secretly, Rachel was glad Sam spoiled her son.

Gladys helped Rachel display her photographs on some easels she'd borrowed from the church library.

"They're wonderful. Who would have thought a rinky-dink town like Finley had so much hidden beauty. I never would have thought black-and-white photos could be so pretty, but it adds an antique look to the pictures." Gladys admired a picture of an old rock well with a wooden bucket surrounded by snow and icicles dripping from the crank overhead. Another photo showed Johnson's meadow dressed in pristine white, the tall elm trees shimmering with frost.

"I hope people like them." Rachel had her doubts.

"Are you kidding? When Emmaline sees this picture of her apple orchard, she'll snap it up quick."

Rachel gazed at the boxes of other items people had brought for the sale. "What can I do to help?"

"You can help me finish laying out the arts and crafts. The crowds will arrive soon."

Rachel found herself immersed in work, setting out some of the most beautiful homemade doilies, baby clothes and quilts she'd ever seen.

As predicted, the room soon filled with people, sampling treats from the baked-goods table, sipping cups of hot wassail or bobbing for apples. They chatted and laughed as they perused the items for sale.

Rachel kept one eye on Danny as he flitted around the room with Charlie and the other children. He participated in the fishing booth, the beanbag toss and face painting. Rachel hummed along with the music blaring over the loudspeaker. As she displayed a handful of homemade dishrags, an unexplainable feeling of warmth rushed over her. Turning, she stared at the double doors and saw Sam standing there watching her. Funny how she sensed him even before she knew he was there.

His expression remained passive, but his eyes smiled as he sauntered over to her. She stood mesmerized, as if they were the only two people in the room. When he reached her, he leaned his head down and spoke low. "Hi, there."

"Hi, Sam. You just getting here?" Okay, not too original, but the best she could muster with her tongue dry as a board.

"Yep. I wanted a chance to bid on your pumpkin bread."

Her mouth dropped open. "How did you know they're going to auction my bread? You just arrived."

He jerked a thumb in the direction of the door. "Fred Baxter told me outside. News spreads fast in this town. But you may hear complaints for only bringing four loaves."

She shook her head. "I can't believe all the fuss. It's just sweet bread."

"Have you tasted your grandmother's bread?"

Okay, enough said. The bread was moist and delicious. To these people, it seemed an old, cherished tradition had returned to town. And that's when she realized how much these people had loved her grandmother. Being a part of this community brought her incredible joy.

"You don't have to bid on my bread, Sam. I'll bring you some tomorrow." She'd made twenty loaves, thinking to give one to Danny's teachers and each of her friends. Of course, her best friends were Sam and Gladys. It did no good to deny it.

"That'd be nice, but I'm definitely going to bid tonight. The money's for a good cause."

His words wrapped around her like a warm blanket and she couldn't help feeling pleased. "I'm glad you're here."

Now, why did she say that?

"It's nice to be here. Except for house calls, I rarely get out much for socializing."

"You don't go out, you don't attend church. What do you do besides work, Sam?" The words were out of her mouth before she could think to pull them back. He'd been awfully good to her and Danny and she had no right to be rude.

He shrugged one muscled shoulder. "That's about it."

"I could fix us dinner at my house on Sunday. I don't have as nice a kitchen as you, but it works fine. You could even take us to church that morning." Okay, she'd just jumped into the deep end of the ocean.

A thoughtful expression tugged at his brows. "You think so?"

"Yes." She bit her bottom lip.

"I'll have to think about it."

His concession was progress.

"Hey! That's me riding Scottie O'Grady."

Rachel turned and saw a thin man with a hawkish nose standing in front of her photographs. He pointed at a picture of the racetrack just outside of town, taken one week after the blizzard hit and the snow started to melt. The scene displayed a lone rider on a sleek horse, loping around the track, both of them covered with mud and slush.

"And those are the two old water barrels out back of my general store and that's my cat." Selma Granger leaned close to inspect the photo, which showed long icicles hanging from the wooden eaves of her store, high above the barrels. A gray cat stood to one side, picking its way across mud puddles in the alley.

"Who took this picture? I want to buy it. Have you got any more?" The horse rider slapped a fifty-dollar bill down on the table.

Selma clicked her purse open. "And I want the picture of my general store. I know just where I'll hang it."

Gladys stood behind the table, smiling happily as she took their money. "Rachel Walker took these photographs."

As she pulled out brown paper bags to wrap the pictures, Gladys pointed at Rachel. Everyone turned to stare at her.

So much for remaining anonymous.

She looked away just as Sam leaned near and whispered close to her ear. "It looks like your photographs are a big hit."

Rachel blinked, more than surprised. She soon found herself surrounded by people asking about the pictures. When had she taken them? Why did she choose that particular view? She smiled and politely answered their questions, pleased that the camera Alex had given her brought so much joy to others.

"Okay, folks, gather round. It's time for the auction," Fred Baxter, the town mayor, called over the loudspeaker.

Martha brought out a beautiful queen-sized quilt draped over her arms. Standing on the stage, Cherise Melahn helped her keep it off the floor as they displayed the intricate pattern on the blue-and-gold-pieced squares.

"Lucille Garvey made this quilt. It's taken her two years to complete, and we're mighty grateful for the donation," Fred announced. "We'll start the bidding at two hundred dollars."

Fred then launched into a rapid-fire auctioneer's voice as he called for bids. Voices rang out and hands shot into the air as everyone tried to get the winning bid. Rachel watched in fascination as the price zoomed to six hundred dollars in a matter of seconds.

Rachel stepped close to Sam and he leaned his head down to hear her whispered words. He smelled nice. "Have you seen Lucille tonight?"

Without drawing attention, he pointed toward the stage where the elderly woman sat in the audience, head held high with pride. When the bidding ended at seven hundred and eighty-five dollars, Lucille beamed with pleasure.

"Oh, no!" Rachel half-wished Lucille hadn't attended the bazaar. Although it was all in good fun, Rachel realized she faced a formidable foe. She shouldn't be so conceited about her pumpkin bread, but she still felt competitive.

"What's the matter?" Sam asked.

"I sure hope my bread tastes all right."

He chuckled and slipped an arm around her shoulders to give her a quick hug. "Don't worry. You're a great cook."

He pulled his arm away, but not before she felt a shot of warmth engulf her entire body. She looked at him, buoyed by his smile of encouragement.

Rachel fidgeted nervously until Susan carried her four loaves of pumpkin bread onstage. Fred leaned close while Susan whispered something to him. Then, microphone in hand, he lifted one loaf of her bread high in the air. "Folks, we have a special treat tonight. I understand this pumpkin bread is Myra Duarte's recipe, made by her granddaughter, Rachel. Before Myra died, this bread won the blue ribbon at the county fair for eight years running. I'll open the bidding at ten dollars a loaf."

Rachel staggered against Sam's side. Ten dollars? Unbelievable!

"You okay?" Sam steadied her.

"Yes, I think so."

Vic Lockhart smiled at Rachel as he raised his hand and offered twenty dollars for one loaf of bread. Rachel watched the proceedings as if from a tunnel, stunned that anyone would pay such an outlandish price for a simple loaf of sweet bread.

"Twenty-one!" Old Mr. Hinkle stood leaning on his walking cane in front of the stage. When Rachel looked at him, he raised one bony hand and winked.

"Two hundred dollars for all four loaves."

Rachel turned and stared at Sam. He didn't look at her, but continued to gaze at Fred, his voice still ringing in the air. Rachel couldn't move. Her ears buzzed. Surely she hadn't heard him right. He had just bid fifty dollars a loaf. For her bread.

"I'll give you two hundred and ten dollars for all four loaves." Dwayne Claridge's strong voice pierced the silence. Cherise hung on the man's arm, giving him a simpering smile. Maybe Cherise had found husband number four. If Sam hadn't interceded and given Rachel a job, she might have become like Cherise. The thought made Rachel's skin crawl.

"And I'll bid two hundred and fifteen," Vic said.

Mr. Hinkle checked his wallet, then shook his head. "Sorry. I'm out."

Rachel felt light-headed, hardly able to believe what was happening. These men were trying to outbid Sam. For her bread.

"Three hundred dollars." Sam spoke without blinking.

"Sam, it's too much," Rachel whispered.

He ignored her.

Vic gave a half-hearted chuckle. "It's for a good cause, but a bit too rich for me."

Dwayne didn't say a word as he glowered at Dr. Thorne.

"Going once. Going twice. Sold!" Fred pointed at Sam. "Four loaves of prize-winning pumpkin bread to Dr. Sam Thorne for the sum of three hundred dollars."

The room buzzed as everyone leaned their heads together to discuss the bidding. Before Sam went to collect his prize, he leaned down and whispered to her. "I think you've just set a new town record."

Rachel stood frozen, vaguely aware of people patting her on the back, congratulating her. Danny came and took her hand, smiling up at her with pride. "That's your bread, Mommy."

"Yes, sweetheart. Mine and Grammy's," she agreed.

After Sam stowed his winnings outside in his truck, Rachel accompanied him as he took Danny and Charlie over to bob apples. She found herself staring at him, completely charmed by his smile and the water dripping from his nose and chin. The boys squealed when he threatened to eat their cupcakes and laughed when he won them each a paper airplane in the bean bag toss. Rachel couldn't remember having so much fun.

Later that evening, everyone left except for the cleanup committee. Danny sagged on a metal chair beside Charlie, both boys worn out from the festivities. Sam helped the other men fold tables and chairs and put them away in the storage closet. While Rachel cleared the tables, she watched him work, thinking how strong and handsome he looked in his dress slacks and blue Western-cut shirt—

She shook her head, wishing she could keep her eyes off him. Her indifference seemed to be getting more difficult to fight.

"You about ready to leave?" Sam startled her when he put the lid on the box of decorations she'd been packing for Gladys.

"Yes, I think so."

"Then I'll walk you to your truck."

Her truck. He said it as though the vehicle belonged to her. She knelt beside Danny, who dozed on his chair.

"Danny, can you wake up for me?" She nudged him, helping him to his feet before threading his arms through the sleeves of his coat and zipping it for him.

"Come here, tiger." Sam scooped the sleepy boy into his arms.

Rachel glanced over at Charlie, who lay curled on the floor, his head resting on his wadded up coat. "Maybe you should help Gladys. She has more stuff to carry."

"She's not quite ready to leave yet. I'll come back after I help you."

Together, they walked out into the night. The chill air felt good after the stuffy interior of the hall. She breathed deeply, looking up at the sky where she saw not a single twinkling star.

"Lots of cloud cover tonight," Sam remarked. "The clouds hold more warmth to the earth so we'll have more melt-off."

At her truck, she dug into her purse for her keys. Most people in Finley rarely locked their vehicles, but she still had the habit.

She opened the door for Sam and he finally secured Danny in the front seat with his seat belt, then closed the door. Sam rounded the truck and opened the door to the driver's seat for Rachel. She got in before turning to look at him.

"Thanks for everything, Sam." She spoke softly, hating to disturb the quiet tranquility of this wonderful evening.

He stepped near, his head level with hers. So close that she could feel his warm breath against her cheek.

"Rach, there isn't much to do in this small town, but I was wondering if maybe you…if you would like to have dinner with me Friday night."

She froze. "You mean, dinner as friends or like a date?"

He ran a hand over his face, considering her words. "Both."

No! she wanted to yell. This was too soon. For all of them. She cared for this man; she couldn't deny it. Yet they both harbored broken hearts, and Danny felt threatened by Sam's presence in their home. Maybe with time, Danny could overcome his resentment. Maybe not at all. But right now, she shouldn't agree to go out with Sam.

"Okay, what time?" Her own words startled her. As if someone else were speaking for her and she was nothing more than a bystander. She tried to tell herself that Sam was too old for her. She still loved Alex. Deeply.

"I'll pick you up at seven." Sam gave her a dazzling smile, then reached out and touched his fingers against her cheek. She felt his warmth against her skin, like rays of sunshine after a year of cloudy skies.

Stepping back, he closed the door and she fired up the engine. As she pulled away, she glanced in her rearview mirror. He stood in the parking lot, lifting his hand to wave farewell. Then, she gripped the steering wheel hard. Alex was gone and she needed to get out more. Perhaps a date with Dr. Thorne was just what she needed. It was time she put aside her grief.

She glanced over at Danny, expecting to find him asleep. He sat hunkered against the door, scowling at her. "You're going out with Sam on a date?"

"If it's okay with you."

He looked straight ahead, considering her words. "You mean you wouldn't go if I asked you not to?"

She shook her head. "Nope. I won't go if you don't want me to."

He stared at the floor, his mouth pursed tight. "Do you want to go out with him?"

"Yes, I do. But that doesn't mean I don't love Daddy. He'll

always be your father and my sweetheart, no matter what. But I don't want to feel sad anymore. I want us to be happy again."

He digested her words for several moments, then turned and stared out the dark window. "It's okay with me."

Her son had given his begrudging permission, yet Rachel felt uncertain. This might be the first step for her and Danny to heal from Alex's death. Or it could become the final death blow to her friendship with Sam.

Chapter Fourteen

He'd really done it this time. After twelve years of heartache, Sam had finally asked another woman out on a date. As he helped turn off the lights and lock up the town hall, he waited for panic to climb up his throat. But it didn't come. Instead, he felt complete peace. He needed this date with Rachel. And from the looks of things, so did she. Both of them single. Both of them lonely.

He said good night to the mayor and then helped his sister to her car. He hoped for Rachel's sake they didn't have another storm coming in. Then, he thought better of it. More snow would give him an excuse to go over to her place to plow her road and driveway. Anything to be near her.

For the first time in a long time, he had a date with a woman. And not just any woman. With Rachel, he could forget his painful loss. He craved someone like her. Craved a second chance. And he envied Alex. Envied the love Rachel still held in her heart for her dead husband. How he wished someone loved him like that. She made him feel like he could see beyond tomorrow. Made him want to do more than just go through the motions of life. He wanted to live again, and he couldn't explain the lightness in his chest.

Ah, who was he kidding? He was too old for her. And out of practice in dealing with a beautiful woman. And too set in his ways to change. Besides, he didn't have room in his life for a woman and her young son.

Of course he did! He had *all* the room in his heart, just waiting for someone like Rachel and Danny to fill up every nook and cranny. It was as if he'd been hurtling toward this moment in time all his life, but now he'd run out of road and didn't know where to go from here.

A spark of danger flashed in his mind. She'd just left him and still he wanted to see her again with a desperation that bordered on crazy. He didn't want to place his heart on a platter for her to carve up. He was too old for that kind of pain again.

Maybe it was already too late.

Sam picked Rachel and Danny up at precisely seven o'clock on Friday night. He was dressed in a navy blue Western-cut suit, and he smelled nice. He'd shaved and slicked his hair back and looked so handsome Rachel had to blink. Standing on her front porch, he presented her with a single red rose.

"A rose! Where on earth did you get it?" Finley had no florist shops, and the deep snow would have killed any fresh flower gardens.

He gave her a dazzling smile. "I ordered it in special from Granger's General Store. You look beautiful in that black velvet dress."

His compliment left her weak-kneed. The past year felt more like a century, and she had a big void inside. Now it seemed Sam had filled that vacancy, and she longed to be much more than friends—

"Let's go." Danny grabbed his coat and brushed between them as he headed outside.

Sam chuckled and jerked his thumb toward the truck. "Looks like Danny's eager to go."

Yes. Rachel sensed her son still didn't like the idea of her dating Sam, even though he'd given his consent.

She got her coat and Sam helped her put it on, then he held her elbow as they walked to the truck. As they drove into town, Danny sat in the back, quiet and subdued. Normally, he bounced on the backseat, excited to spend time at Charlie's house since Gladys had agreed to babysit.

"What are you and Charlie gonna do tonight?" Sam asked.

Danny gave an impatient sigh. "Play video games. Gladys is making pizza and popcorn for Charlie and me. She said we can stay up late since it's the weekend."

"That sounds fun."

"You goin' to the diner?" The boy sounded worried.

"Nope," Sam said.

"Then, where you goin'?"

Rachel smiled, waiting for Sam to respond. In Finley, they could go to Claridge's Diner or stay home and cook. Knowing how Sam felt about Dwayne, she suspected he'd take her to his house for a home-cooked meal. She didn't mind. She loved being at Sam's place. So did her son, although she doubted he'd admit it right now.

Sam glanced at Danny in his rearview mirror and grinned. "It's none of your business, pal. You'll just have to wait until your mom gets home to find out where I took her."

Danny gave a little huff and showed a pout. "Just don't keep my mom out too late."

Sam looked startled, then recovered. "Don't worry, Danny. I would never do anything to hurt you or your mom."

The boy frowned, thinking this over. He scowled out the

window, keeping his silence for the remainder of the trip. After dropping Danny off, Rachel wasn't surprised when Sam headed for his place. She gripped the armrest and looked at him, remembering Gladys telling her that Sam couldn't cook. "So, you're the chef tonight?"

"Yep. I hope you enjoy it." He reached out and squeezed her hand, holding it as he drove along.

His small gesture caused Rachel's heart to beat faster. Right then, she didn't care if their meal was burnt to a crisp. Instead, she enjoyed the warmth of his rough hands, his manly strength mingled with gentleness. She looked out the window as the darkness sped past. The headlights on Sam's truck showed the way as they turned off onto the dirt road. He ran the heater and she settled back against the seat, being patient.

"Won't dinner be burned by the time we arrive?"

"Nope. Gladys told me what to do with the Crock-Pot. I've timed this perfectly."

Crock-Pot? Rachel wondered if Gladys had prepared the meal and brought it to Sam, keeping it warm until they were ready to eat.

"What are we having?"

"You'll see."

"You're really not going to tell me until we get there?"

"What can I say? I'm a man of mystery." His lips twitched with a suppressed smile.

She chuckled, enjoying his sense of humor and the momentary secrecy. It'd been a long time since a man thought enough to plan a special evening just for her, and she found herself enjoying it to the hilt.

As they pulled into the yard at Sam's place, Rachel unbuckled her seat belt and looked at the house. The porch light was on. The tall post looming over the driveway sprayed light across the front of the barn. Sam got out of the truck and came around to open the door for her. After he helped her out, he took her hand and led her up the walkway.

Inside the warm house, the delicious aroma of pot roast engulfed them. The living room looked tidy, the carpets streaked with vacuum marks. Rachel stared at the floor, hardly able to believe Sam had cooked and cleaned for her.

He hung their coats in the hall closet, then took her hand and led her to the formal dining room. Two tall, tapered candles sat in the middle of the long table covered with a white linen tablecloth and napkins. Rachel recognized the dainty pink flower pattern on the plates. "You borrowed Gladys's china?"

"Nothing but the best. It was our mother's china." He struck a match and leaned over to light the candles. "Sorry I don't have a nice centerpiece. I didn't think about that when I ordered the rose from Granger's General Store."

"You didn't need to go to all this trouble. We could have gone to the diner in town, or I could have cooked for us."

"No, I wanted our first date to be special. Gladys told me what to do, but I prepared everything myself."

"I'm impressed. Your table looks beautiful."

Beaming with pleasure, Sam held Rachel's chair so she could sit.

"I'll be right back." He disappeared into the kitchen.

"Can I help?"

"Not tonight," he called over his shoulder.

He returned momentarily with a breadbasket and used his hand to place a fluffy dinner roll on each of their plates. He then presented a bottle of nonalcoholic apple cider. "I have ice water, but I thought we might like to toast the evening."

"Yes, thank you." She held up both of their glasses.

Sam poured the bubbly beverage over ice, then brought them each a delicious garden salad with creamy dressing on the side. She felt odd being idle while he bustled around to serve her. When he sat close beside her, they ate and talked about inconsequential things: the snow, their patients at the clinic, and Danny.

"I thought we were getting along pretty well. But lately, he doesn't seem to like me much," Sam said.

"It's not that. He obviously adores you, Sam. He just thinks you might be trying to take his father's place."

Sam considered the golden liquid in his glass. "Maybe I need to tell him that's not my goal."

Rachel prayed it was that simple.

"He loves Blackie. Why don't you let him have the dog? She's old enough to leave her momma now," Sam offered.

"I don't think so. You of all people know I'm not very good with dogs."

"Yes you are, Rachel. You don't give yourself enough credit. My office has never been so organized. You've got the financials in order for the first time in years. And calling to remind our patients when they're supposed to come in has really cut down on missed appointments. And Danny's learned how to feed and care for Blackie. He knows what to do."

"Until she does something messy in the house. No thanks." She smiled and shook her head, but his praise warmed her heart.

"So, let her live outside. Shadow and Tabitha live in the barn, and Blackie's used to it. As long as she has a dry place out of the wind, she'll make Danny a good pet."

He leaned near, his eyes glittering in the candle glow as he smiled. Ah, she felt lost in their depths.

"You know there are a lot of advantages to having a dog at your place." His smile stole her breath.

"Such as?" She stared at his lips.

"Well, for one thing, they warn you when something's wrong. And they chase off intruders."

Hmm. A dog might be good to have around to chase off wild coyotes and other varmints. Maybe having a dog wouldn't be so bad. "I'll think about it."

"Would you like the next course?" He stood and removed their salad plates. Within minutes, he brought them each a dish of tender pot roast, potatoes and gravy, and thin baby carrots glazed with honey sauce.

"Wow! You must have been cooking all day. Everything is delicious."

He smiled big, looking pleased. By the time they finished their dessert of crème brulee with raspberries and cream, Rachel was stuffed. She stood and walked into the kitchen, planning to help with the dishes. Her eyes widened and her mouth dropped open at what she saw. His meal had been delectable, but the kitchen looked like it had exploded with dirty pots and pans. Gravy had been slopped on the stove. Dishes filled the stainless steel sink.

Rachel chuckled, then took a deep breath and looked around for an apron. "I can help clean up."

"Oh, no you don't. I'll take care of this mess later." He took her arm and steered her back toward the living room.

"Really, I don't mind helping," Rachel offered.

Sam wrapped his arm around her waist and led her to the sofa. "Not tonight. Tell me about yourself."

Without intending to, she told him how she'd met and married Alex and how devastated she'd been when he died. "We met eight years ago in a restaurant where I was waitressing. We fell head over teakettle in love and married way too young."

"Do you think you can ever love again?" he asked, as she looked into his eyes.

"Yes." The word slipped out before she could stop it.

He breathed a deep sigh and she realized he'd been holding his breath.

"And what about you?" she asked.

"There's not much to tell."

"Is that Melanie?" She indicated a picture of him standing between a younger Gladys and another woman with reddish-gold hair. He was smiling and happy.

He looked away and his mouth tightened. "Yes. I was such a fool in those days. Young, stupid and selfish. Melanie wanted me to become a hotshot medical doctor and move to San Diego, where she grew up. She didn't care about family or setting down roots. But I had different ideas. I wanted babies. Lots and lots of kids. I wanted to be a veterinarian and move back here to Finley and set up a small practice and help all the ranchers in the area. That wasn't grand enough for Melanie. She liked high society, not country life."

Rachel stilled, wondering what really happened the night Melanie died.

"We had a terrible fight," Sam explained. "She broke off our engagement. She said she didn't love me anymore and I was holding her back from the life she wanted. I lost my temper and said things I've regretted ever since. Cruel words that broke her heart. In her anger, Melanie grabbed the steering wheel and I lost control of the car."

Rachel cringed, listening intently. He blinked his eyes fast and turned his face away. "I could forgive myself for a simple car accident, but I haven't been able to forgive what I said to her that night. If only I could take it all back, I'd pull off to the side of the road and talk calmly to her for a while. Maybe we weren't meant to be together, but I didn't need to hurt her the way I did. If I'd been kinder with my words, Melanie might still be alive—"

Rachel bit her lip, wishing he hadn't told her. She could just imagine the spiteful words they must have said to one another. Her heart went out to them both for the price they'd paid for their cruelty to each other. "I'm sorry, Sam."

"I don't want your pity, Rachel. I just want to be part of your life. Family means everything to me, but for the longest time I feared I'd never get a second chance. Then you came into my life and helped me believe in myself again. You taught me to forgive myself and to trust in the Lord. You remind me of everything good and beautiful in the world. I didn't dare take a chance on love again. Until you."

Sam's eyes burned into hers. She definitely understood his fear. As he took her hand, her defenses crashed to the ground. She loved Alex and had struggled to let him go. Now, she finally had the strength to take that leap of faith.

"Do you think I'm an evil man because of what I've told you?" he asked.

She reached up and touched his face with her fingertips. "Of course not, Sam. You're human. We all lose our temper and say things we regret later on. The Lord wouldn't want you to torture yourself like this."

"I think that's true for you, too."

"What do you mean?"

"You can trust me, Rachel. I'd never hurt you or Danny." He hugged her close, then leaned forward and placed a gentle kiss on her lips. For several magical moments, she felt giddy and beautiful. As her gaze locked with his, she leaned her head against his shoulder, feeling warm and safe.

"I planned dinner *and* a movie for us," he said.

"Oh?"

He reached for a handful of DVDs sitting on the coffee table. "I borrowed these from Gladys. Pick which one you'd like to watch."

She scanned the selections and laughed. "Wow! I'm impressed."

He quirked one eyebrow.

"All of these are chick flicks. You sure you're up for that?"

"Gladys said you'd like them."

"I do, thank you." His thoughtfulness impressed her even more. She handed him a movie, then watched as he stood and popped it into the DVD player. He returned to the sofa, wrapping one arm around her shoulders while he used the remote control to turn on the movie, a sappy love story about a lonely widower and his young son who find true love with a sensitive woman.

Rachel settled against Sam, enjoying herself as the movie progressed. Within fifteen minutes, Sam fell asleep. She didn't mind. She felt comfortable and domestic, curled against this strong, considerate man. Even as her heartache seemed to disappear, she prayed her son could accept her loving Sam.

Chapter Fifteen

The following Monday, when Rachel returned to work, she walked to her desk, stowed her purse away in a drawer, then turned and froze. Hanging on the wall in the waiting room were five of her photographs from the bazaar fund-raiser.

"You like them?"

She tilted her head and found Sam standing behind her. Meeting her gaze, he leaned against the doorjamb, looking lean and handsome in a pair of faded blue jeans and scuffed cowboy boots. He wore a blue smock over his denim shirt, his arms folded across his chest.

"You bought my pictures?" A lump formed in her throat.

"I did. They look nice, don't they?"

"You spent way too much money at the bazaar, Sam."

"I love the pictures. Shorty said we cleared enough money to begin the electrical work on the town hall. Of course, both of us are donating a lot of our own time to the cause."

"That's great." She wasn't surprised, knowing Sam freely gave of his time and service to other people.

She couldn't help feeling flattered that he'd bought her photographs. She hung up her coat, no longer wanting to fight her growing attraction for this man. Life seemed so simple here in Finley. She hadn't felt this peaceful since before Alex died. In reality, her life was quite complicated.

When she turned to face him again, he was gone. For most of the day, she kept her distance from him. She needed to figure out how to deal with Danny's misgivings. Gladys must have sensed her withdrawn mood. "Is everything okay between you and Sam?"

"Of course."

"Good. I thought you two were getting along so well and I don't want anything to spoil it."

Rachel gripped the stapler by the copy machine. Her magical evening with Sam had ended and she didn't want to return to reality. She could let go of her grief and move on with her life, but she wasn't so certain about her son.

She turned and walked away before Gladys could ask more questions. Maybe happily ever after didn't really exist. Not for her.

That evening after work, Sam took both boys over to Rachel's house, babysitting while she and Gladys attended a PTA meeting in town. He would have taken the boys to his house, but Rachel told him about a floorboard in her bedroom she kept tripping over and he intended to repair the problem.

"I want to go check on Blackie. She has a cold," Danny told him, as they drove along the dirt road to Rachel's place.

"Not tonight. I need to make some repairs and fix you boys some dinner."

"Charlie and I can walk over by ourselves."

Sam shook his head as he pulled his truck into the driveway and killed the engine. "No, your mom wouldn't like that. It's getting late and it's too cold. I'll take care of Blackie for you, so don't worry."

"But what if she's really sick? What if she dies?" The boy's voice trembled.

Sam wished Rachel would agree to give the dog to Danny for his birthday. "Blackie's not that sick."

Disbelief filled Danny's eyes. "That's what you said about the mother cat, and look what happened to her."

Okay, Sam admitted he'd been wrong about the cat, but she'd been old. He'd done what he could for the animal. He just wished he could have done more. Now, he was at a loss how to regain Danny's trust. "I'm sorry, but I have no doubt that mother cat is running around in heaven with your daddy."

Danny's brow crinkled. "You mean it? Daddy's got my cat?"

"I'm sure of it."

A smile tugged at the corners of Danny's mouth. "Then, that's okay. Dad won't be alone up in heaven any more."

Sam patted the boy's shoulder. "That's right. And if your mom agrees, you can visit Blackie tomorrow."

"But I want to go now."

"No, not tonight."

"You're not my boss." The boy showed a mutinous frown.

Sam froze, taken off guard by the boy's resentful glare. "I'm sorry, but I'm the boss tonight, son."

"I'm not your son." Danny bit out the words, then scurried out of the truck, followed by Charlie.

Sam sat in the driver's seat, stinging. He cared for Danny and wondered how to overcome the boy's animosity. Knowing Danny's rebellion stemmed from his fear for Blackie, Sam shook it off. Instead, he thought of the gift he had for Rachel, hidden beneath the tarp in the back of his truck. She'd be so surprised. He could just imagine her emotions when she saw what he'd done for her. He hoped it made her smile.

After retrieving his red toolbox from the back of his truck, he went inside the house with the boys. The living room smelled of cinnamon, cloves and pine needles. Sugar cookies sat stacked on the kitchen counter, waiting to be frosted. Photographs in simple wood frames hung on the walls. An orange-and-brown afghan covered the back of the threadbare sofa. In spite of the meager furnishing, the room felt calm and inviting. Peaceful. How he wished this was his home to share with Rachel and Danny. He decided then to give her a hefty raise. And a bonus wouldn't hurt, either.

As Sam made his way down the hall, he passed by Danny's room. The door was closed, but he heard the boys' low voices within. Subdued voices. Not what he usually heard when they got together. No doubt, Danny was still worried about his dog.

In the master bedroom, Sam picked up Rachel's Bible on the bedside table. The book lay open to Psalms 3 and he read several passages. He thought of her slender hands holding this book as she sought God's words. Small hands, but willing to serve.

Rachel said he should give the Lord a second chance. It'd been a long time since he'd talked to his Heavenly Father. Rachel seemed so certain God loved sinners. Even him. Still, Sam couldn't quite accept her Pollyanna attitude. Frankly, he didn't know how to pray anymore. Over the years, his relationship with God had dwindled to nothing, and he doubted he could get it back.

So, where did that leave him and Rachel? She wanted a man who loved the Lord, no doubt about it. And he couldn't seem to be that kind of man for her.

But he wanted to.

He set his toolbox on the floor beside the closet, then removed a hammer and nails. Wedging the straight edge of the hammer between the wooden planks on the floor, he pried up the rusty nail. He'd get this repaired and Rachel wouldn't trip over it anymore. He liked doing things for her. Fixing up her drafty old house so she and Danny would be more comfortable. But deep inside, he couldn't help wishing she was his wife and Danny was his son and they lived with him. For years, his heart had been empty and aching. Now, he considered giving God a second chance.

How should he begin? Maybe talking to the Lord in prayer was a good start. And maybe a visit to church on Sunday wouldn't hurt. He needed the companionship of his congregation to get back on his feet with his Heavenly Father.

Hmm. He'd think about it.

"Come on, Charlie. Go with me." Danny sat on his bed, trying to convince Charlie to go with him over to Sam's barn.

What if Blackie died and he never got to say goodbye? Just like Daddy. The thought made his chest feel heavy and he couldn't breathe for several seconds. Kind of like the time he fell off the teeter-totter at school and had the wind knocked out of him.

"No, Uncle Sam said to stay here." Charlie didn't look up at him as he pushed two Matchbox cars around on the carpet. Danny knew he was thinking about it, though. He could tell by the way Charlie kept looking at the closed door. As if he feared they might get caught.

"But we can run over to Sam's house, check on Blackie, and be back before anyone knows we're gone."

"Face it, Danny. Your mom's never gonna let you have a dog. She hates dogs."

Danny's shoulders stiffened and he picked up Stripe, who lay curled on his pillow. Holding the kitten in his lap, he stroked her soft fur. He didn't blame Mom for hating dogs. Not after she told him what happened when she was just his age. But he sure wished she'd get over her fear. "Don't say that. She let us keep Stripe. Mom will come around to letting me have Blackie, you'll see."

"But Uncle Sam said not to go. He'd be mighty mad if we disobeyed. So would our moms."

Danny set Stripe aside, smiling as the kitten yawned and stretched. He had more important work to do right now. "Our moms will never know if you don't tell them. Let's go. We won't stay very long."

"I don't know." Charlie frowned, and Danny realized he was losing ground.

"If we cross the pond, it'll take half the time and we'd be there and back before you know it."

"But Uncle Sam said never to go out on the ice, even if it looks frozen solid."

Danny shrugged. "It looks firm enough to me."

Charlie pursed his lips. "Uncle Sam says the ice is thinner than it looks."

"What if we test it out first? If it's too dangerous, we can always walk around, can't we?"

"Well—"

"Ah, come on, sissy. It'll be easy. No one will know."

Sissy. The word every boy in second grade hated more than girls. Still, Charlie didn't look convinced. But Danny knew just what to do to get his way with his best friend. "Please, Charlie? I'll give you my new comic book."

He hated to give up his Rocketman comic book, but these were desperate times. Charlie heaved a big sigh and smiled, plumping his freckled cheeks. Danny knew he had him now. Charlie couldn't tell him no. Not when he knew how much Danny loved Blackie and wished he could bring the dog home with him. In the meantime, Danny had to know Blackie was safe. He had to see his dog. If anything happened and he never got to say goodbye, Danny would never forgive himself. He had to go.

* * *

Sam stood at the kitchen sink, draining the boxed macaroni and cheese he had just prepared for the boys' dinner. He glanced at the clock, anxious for Rachel to get home. She wouldn't believe what he had found beneath the floorboards in her bedroom. He couldn't believe it, either.

The unmistakable sound of Shadow's shrill barking came from outside, back behind the house. What was his dog doing over on this side of the pond? Shadow should be home, warm and safe in the barn.

Walking to the living room, Sam flipped on the porch light and opened the front door. He stepped outside, listening. As he tilted his head to one side, he noticed the increased cold without the sun's warming rays.

Yes, definitely Shadow's bark. He sounded upset, like when he warned Sam a stranger had come to visit. Shaking his head, Sam closed the door. What had gotten into the dog? Probably found a rabbit.

Sam stirred the powdered cheese in with the pasta, then set the pan on the table. As he got the milk out of the refrigerator, he called to the boys, "Danny! Charlie! Come and eat."

He placed a bowl of hot string beans beside the pasta. Not much of a meal, but he'd at least thought of a vegetable for the boys. Rachel would like that.

They didn't respond. "Come on, guys. Food's getting cold."

The dog continued to bark. As soon as the boys sat down to eat, he'd go out and see what was wrong.

Walking down the hallway, he knocked on the door to Danny's room. No response.

"Boys! Come eat." He opened the door…and stared at the empty room. The curtains billowed as cold air blew through the open window. When he leaned over the windowsill, Sam saw two sets of footprints in the snow, leading around back.

"Those little stinkers."

They'd disobeyed him and snuck out of the house. And he knew exactly where they were headed. Over to his place to visit Blackie. No wonder Shadow was barking down by the pond.

A sense of foreboding gripped him. No, the boys wouldn't dare—

He raced to the kitchen where he jerked open the utility drawer, looking for the flashlight he knew Rachel kept there. Outside, he ran along the walk path to the back of the house. He sprayed the beam of the flashlight across the ground. Farther out, Shadow stood on the shore, barking. Out on the pond, Sam could make out two dark shapes—

His heartbeat accelerated, and a tremor of fear washed over him. A faint cry reached his ears and he broke into a mad sprint toward the pond. As he hurried down the gentle slope, his booted feet sank deep into the snowdrifts. He inhaled drafts of cold air, his breath rushing out like puffs of smoke from a chimney.

"Hang on! I'm coming," he yelled, almost there.

"It's Sam." Danny's voice sounded hoarse, like he'd been screaming for help.

Sam reached the shore and assessed the situation, looking around for a solution. Danny lay flat on his stomach on the cold ice, gripping Charlie's wrists as the other boy clung to the edge where he'd fallen through. Even in the pale light, both boys' faces looked ashen, their eyes wide with fear.

"Hurr-hurry!" Charlie barely got the word out between his lips.

If Sam went out to them, his weight would break the ice. He'd fall through and they all would drown. "Hang on, boys. Just hang on."

Danny shuddered as icy water washed over the side of the breakage, soaking his clothes. "I won't let...let go. I...I promise."

Hypothermia. If Sam didn't get them out soon—

Think! Think!

Please, Heavenly Father. Please help me save these boys. If You truly love us, then help me now. Help me find a way.

Sam prayed over and over again for the first time in years. And then, a picture filled his mind with such clarity that he knew what to do.

The boat! He ran to the craft, moored to the dock and land-locked by ice.

There! Reaching inside, he lifted an oar, then traced the boys' footsteps out on the ice, moving slow but urgently. He followed their path a short ways before he lay down on the ice and stretched out to disburse his weight.

"No, Sam! You—you'll fall through li-like Charlie," Danny croaked, and he shuddered.

Sam had no choice. In a leap of faith, he put all of their lives in God's hands.

Please, Lord, don't let me fall through. Don't let us die. Hold us in the hollow of Thy hand.

Sam dragged the oar with him, scooting closer to the boys. The wind blew past, freezing him to the core. A cold that settled in his bones and made him wonder if he'd ever be warm again. He should have grabbed his coat before he left the house. He could only imagine how the boys must feel, lying in the frigid waters of the pond.

As he moved nearer, Sam couldn't explain the calm that filled him. He had no doubt God was there with them, guiding him. Holding up his weight so he didn't crash through the ice. "Danny, stay on your belly and move very slowly over to me. Charlie, you take hold of the oar. Come on, you can do it."

As the two boys thrashed around, cold water sloshed over the edge of broken ice, splashing Sam in the face. He couldn't see well through the darkness. The cold made his hands stiff and numb so his movements became clumsy.

Danny helped Charlie grip the leather thong on the narrow end of the oar.

"That's it, Charlie. Now, hoist yourself up."

"I—I can't." Charlie said. He was shivering—a good sign the hypothermia hadn't progressed to a deadly state. Yet.

"Yes, you can," Sam encouraged. "As soon as you get out of that water, I'm going to carry you home. We'll get you warm. Do it. Now!"

"C-Come on, Charlie. I'll help." Danny tugged on Charlie's arms.

In a gargantuan effort, Charlie pulled himself out of the water. The boys lay there on the ice, their breath wheezing in and out, their small bodies shivering so hard that Sam feared they might break the ice again. While Danny inched his way over to him, Sam reeled in Charlie with the oar. When they reached the shore, they all collapsed in the snow and bushes, breathing harshly, barely able to move.

Get up! Move right now! You don't have much time.

Sam heard the words as if someone spoke directly into his ear. He had to get them inside. He had to get them warm.

He stumbled to his feet, his teeth chattering, his hands fumbling around as he reached for the boys. He picked them both up, carrying one child in each arm. The boys cried, but Sam didn't stop to comfort them. Not until he could get them home.

He staggered beneath their weight, but forced his legs to keep moving. Their wet clothing soaked into his, and his arms trembled like wet noodles. He ignored the pain and pushed on. Their lives depended on him, and he couldn't let them or their mothers down.

He tottered across the field toward the bright lights of

Rachel's house. Shadow rushed ahead, barking, tail high in the air. What a wonderful, noisy dog. If Sam hadn't heard him—

"We're almost there. Almost home." Sam murmured the words over and over, to encourage the boys and himself not to quit.

As they reached the house, headlights flared in the driveway. Gladys parked her car and she and Rachel got out, looking astonished by their appearance. Then they rushed over to help.

Gladys reached him first and took Charlie into her arms. Sam held Danny, hurrying toward the house. The boy clung to him, his little body shaking, his breath rasping from his chest. Sam clenched his jaw. His heart pounded and shattering waves of emotion washed over him as he hugged the boy tighter. He never planned to love this child, but he did. More than he could comprehend. If either of the boys had died tonight—

"What happened?" Rachel took Danny into her arms and pounded up the steps to the front porch.

"Charlie fell through the ice." Sam dragged open the door, holding it while the women went inside.

"The ice? What were they doing out on the pond?" Rachel's voice sounded frantic.

Sam avoided the question. He didn't want to explain his own negligence. Yes, the boys disobeyed him, but they were only seven years old. He should have been more aware of Danny's need to see Blackie. He should have been alert and watched the kids more carefully.

In Danny's room, they worked together to get the boys warm. The women took charge, removing the children's wet clothing and wrapping them in heavy quilts from head to toe.

"Sam, your hands are bleeding," Gladys observed.

He looked down and found his palms covered in thick splinters. He hadn't even noticed the stinging pain until now. "It must have been the oar."

Rachel nodded toward the hallway. "There's tweezers and antiseptic in the bathroom."

Sam took care of himself, cranking up the heat before he pulled out the splinters, applied ointment and wrapped gauze around his injuries. While the women stayed with the children, he heated milk on the stove, then offered the warm liquid to the boys one sip at a time. "I'd call 911, but the nearest EMT is in Elko, almost two hours away."

"What about Doc Greene?" Gladys suggested, as she rubbed her hands briskly over Charlie's arms and legs.

Sam stood in front of the sofa where each woman cradled their son in their arms, the boys swaddled like Eskimos. Their faces had regained a bit more healthy color. "I'm afraid he's out of town. Gone to Sacramento to visit his daughter and her family."

Sam remembered when Rachel literally crashed into his life. They'd made do without a medical doctor then, too. Such was the life of country folk living in a remote Nevada town.

"How could you let this happen?" Rachel asked, her voice soft and filled with censure.

He blinked. "I'm sorry. I thought they were in Danny's room playing."

She didn't look at him and his heart squeezed hard.

"It's not Sam's fault, Mommy. I—I disobeyed 'cause I wanted to see if Blackie was all right. Sam told us we couldn't go, but I convinced Charlie to sneak out my bedroom window." Tears of remorse slid down Danny's ashen cheeks. Sam didn't have the heart to be angry or reprimand the child.

"You look like a frozen popsicle." Charlie showed a stiff smile, his lips tinged with a hint of pink instead of blue.

Danny smiled back and Sam couldn't help thinking how easily children forgave one another. If only Rachel could forgive him. If only he could forgive himself.

"How long was Charlie in the water?" Gladys asked.

"Hours!" Charlie exclaimed. "I've never been so cold. We screamed, but Sam couldn't hear us. Then Shadow came and started barking."

Sam sank into a recliner, resting his injured hands on the arm rests. He breathed deep, relieved now the danger had passed. It must have seemed like hours to the frightened boys. "Thank goodness I heard Shadow. But I figure the boys weren't in the water more than fifteen minutes."

"I'm sure glad you saved us," Danny said.

Sam's throat constricted. "Me, too. I'm grateful I found you and Charlie in time."

Rachel pressed her cheek against Danny's and Sam sensed her detachment. If only he could explain what happened out on the ice. How could he when he didn't understand it himself? The brief flash of intelligence that filled his entire being as he stood out by the pond wondering how to save the boys. Powerful and undeniable, with no questions needing to be asked. The knowledge that God had answered his prayer left him humbled. He didn't know what to think. He only knew what he felt.

Peace and exquisite joy.

Turning away, he brushed the moisture from his eyes, not wanting the women to witness his emotions. He had felt God's presence with him tonight and he longed to savor the sweetness a little while longer before he shared it with anyone else.

Out of the corners of his eyes, Sam caught the frown on Rachel's face and he knew the worst was yet to come.

Chapter Sixteen

An hour later, Rachel came out of Danny's room holding two thermometers. "The boys are sleeping peacefully and their body temps have returned to normal."

Sam stood in the hallway, his battered hands by his sides. Rachel sensed his confusion as he followed her into the kitchen. A myriad of emotions washed over her and she wondered how to tell him what was on her mind.

She took a deep breath. "Gladys is staying here with us tonight. She doesn't want to move Charlie out into the cold night air until she's sure he's okay. She's with the boys now. We'll take turns watching over them through the night and call if we need you."

She wished he'd take the hint and leave. For some reason, his presence reminded her of all she'd lost and what she still could lose.

After washing the thermometers with warm, soapy water, she rinsed them in alcohol.

"How can I help?" Sam asked.

He sounded lost and forlorn, but she couldn't bring herself to speak any words of consolation to salve his conscience right now. Not until she was certain Danny would be okay. "I think you've done enough."

He looked away and his shoulders slumped. "I didn't know they'd snuck out of the house, Rachel. I had no idea what they were up to until I heard Shadow barking out by the pond."

"I know. It wasn't your fault." And she meant it. This wasn't Sam's fault. It just happened.

"Then what?"

"I'm just upset and worried tonight. It's just that—"

"What?"

"I lost my husband a year ago, Sam. I almost lost my son tonight. Can you understand how that makes me feel?"

"Yes, I understand only too well."

No doubt he was thinking of Melanie.

"Look, Rachel, I'll say this once and never again. I lost someone I loved very deeply. It nearly destroyed me. For years, I blamed myself. But something happened tonight out on that pond that I can't quite explain. I just don't feel the same anymore."

"I don't understand."

"I prayed for help for the first time in twelve years and the Lord answered me. I gave up on the Lord years ago, but I now realize He never gave up on me. He's always been there, waiting for me to return to Him. I finally feel free."

"I'm glad, Sam. I'm so happy you've finally forgiven yourself and the Lord." She knew how much Sam had suffered with grief and guilt. But what if Danny had died tonight? He was all she had left, and she didn't know how to overcome his animosity toward Sam.

"But?" he pressed.

"I don't know what you want."

"I want you and Danny. Can't you give us a try, Rachel? That's all I'm asking."

She bit her bottom lip, worried about her son and his shattered feelings. "I don't know. You—"

She bit her tongue to keep from finishing her thought. Somehow, if she didn't say the words out loud, they wouldn't be real.

"Rach, the boys are gonna be okay." He touched her hand, his voice gentle. "What's really bothering you?"

"You! You're not—"

"I'm not what?" He tilted his head to one side, waiting.

She bit her tongue, fighting back the burn of tears.

"I'm not Alex?" he finished for her.

"Yes! I mean, no." She groaned, putting her face in her hands. "Oh, I don't know what I mean anymore."

He moved closer, sitting on the edge of his seat, taking her hands into his. "Then, stop fighting it so much. Just let us happen."

Us?

She'd been an *us* with Alex. They'd been a family when Danny was born. But she couldn't jeopardize Danny's well-being. He'd been through too much already.

"You know, you've taught me something I never believed possible," Sam said.

She brushed at her eyes, her voice heavy with emotion. "And what is that?"

"That it's possible to love more than once. The love we have in our heart can grow and grow. I never thought I could love anyone after Melanie. I've been hiding out, buried in my work, pretending I don't want or need anyone."

"But you share your life with Gladys and Charlie. You have a family. You're not alone."

"It's not the same, and you know it." He took gentle hold of her arms and her breath caught in her throat. "I'm talking about the love between a man and a woman as they build a life together. Without you in my life, they might as well turn off the sun and all the stars in the sky and stop the earth from rotating, because my world would cease to exist."

She took a sharp inhale. No one had ever said such a thing to her. Not even Alex. Oh, how she wanted to wrap her arms around this man and tell him she loved him, too. But she couldn't do it. Not after tonight, when she almost lost her son. "Sam, I don't think this is going to work."

"How do you know unless we try?"

"It's too soon for Danny." The room closed in on her. He wanted her to commit to a relationship and she didn't believe she could.

"My feelings won't change. When is the right time, Rach?"

"That depends on Danny." The hurt in his eyes nearly broke her heart. She hated causing him pain, but she couldn't hurt her son anymore. They'd reached the breaking point. "I'm sorry, Sam."

He looked away, toward the black, vacant window. "Rachel, I'll wait forever if I have to, because I'm crazy about you. But I can't compete with a dead man. I'm not asking you and Danny to stop loving Alex, and I'm not asking you to forget what you shared with him or pretend he isn't Danny's father. I'm just asking you to let me share your life. I'm asking you to let me love you, too."

He stood and walked to the door, pausing there, resting one bandaged hand on the door knob as he turned to look at her from over his shoulder. "When I repaired the floorboard, I found something you'd like to see. I left it on your bed. I think your grandmother wanted you to have it."

He left, wearing his coat over his damp clothes. She almost called him back, thinking she should drive him home. He'd catch pneumonia walking in the cold.

She shook her head, letting him go. If she stopped him, she

might take back her words. And where would that leave Danny? Her son must be her first priority even above her own feelings for Sam.

Standing, she walked down the hallway, careful not to disturb Gladys and the boys. In her bedroom, she clicked on the light, her gaze scanning the room. She took a sharp inhale. Sitting in one corner was her damaged rocking chair, completely restored. She thought Sam had thrown the chair away. Instead, he must have taken it home to his workshop and repaired it.

Tears blurred her vision as she knelt down to inspect the spokes. The grain matched perfectly where the wood had once been splintered. She ran her fingers over the surface, finding it smooth as glass. She couldn't even tell the chair had been damaged. Sam had done this for her. He'd repaired her broken chair just as he'd repaired her broken heart.

Looking up, she saw an old tin box resting in the middle of her bed. She stood and the mattress bounced as she sat on one corner and opened the lid to the box, then gasped.

She pressed her hands to her mouth, staring at tidy stacks of money. Crisp, new bills preserved inside the tin box. She blinked, unable to believe her eyes. After several heart-pounding moments, she picked up one stack of money, and the oxidized rubber band fell apart in her hand. She fanned the bills with her thumb, seeing a few twenties and fifties, but mostly hundred-dollar bills.

A quick perusal of the other stacks led her to scramble over to her desk where she got out a pad of paper and pencil. She quickly tallied her computations and her breath froze in her throat. She could hardly move, dazed by the realization of what had been hidden in Grammy's house all these years.

Almost five hundred thousand dollars.

Oh, Grammy! What were you thinking to keep this kind of money hidden in the house?

Grammy never trusted banks. She'd often told Rachel to replace the flooring after her death. Now, Rachel understood why. She had wanted Rachel to discover the tin box. The realization that this money had rested beneath the floorboards of this old house for the past who-knew-how-many years made Rachel shudder. What if there'd been a fire?

She hid the box in the bottom of her closet, buried beneath piles of shoes. In the morning, she'd go straight to the bank and open a savings account.

And then she realized what this meant. How it could change her and Danny's lives. No more scrimping and doing without. No more pinching every dime just so she could afford food for the table. She could leave Finley if she wanted to. She could take Danny and go anywhere she wanted without worries.

Without Sam.

The thought made her stop. She couldn't imagine life without Dr. Samuel Thorne being there. She walked to the bedroom window and peered out past the frost-covered glass pane, looking at the darkness down by the pond. A shape moved beyond the shore. A tall, strong figure of a man walking fast.

Sam.

Turning away, she heaved a sigh. She should have driven him home in her truck. His truck.

The money didn't change her feelings toward Sam. She loved him. It wasn't his fault the boys fell through the ice. Somehow, they had to help Danny heal from the loss of his father. She knew he liked Sam. Surely she could help him see that Sam didn't mean to usurp his father.

And just like that, she realized the pain she'd carried with her constantly for the past year since Alex died didn't seem quite as heavy. In fact, it seemed quite light, replaced by the knowledge that she could go on loving Alex even while she loved Sam and his dry sense of humor, his intelligence and the way he frolicked with her son in the snow.

This new awareness made her heart take wing. She sank down on the bed, her mind absorbing the reality of her love like the earth soaking up rain. In the morning, she'd find a way to tell Sam. Together, they'd find a way to help Danny over his grief.

Sam's feet crunched through the crusted snow as he crossed the field to his place. Shadow followed, trotting beside him, panting. Inside, Sam's heart and mind screamed.

He'd let Rachel down when the boys snuck out the window and almost died on the ice. Yeah, it could have happened to anyone, but it didn't. It happened to them. And it could have been tragic. How could he make Rachel realize she could trust him now? How could he convince her that she and Danny were safe with him?

After taking Shadow to the barn, he stepped up onto his front porch and stomped the snow off his boots. In spite of his soggy clothes, he barely felt the cold as he opened the door and stepped inside. Hanging his coat on a peg by the door, he pulled his boots off one by one. The gauze on his hands inhibited his movements, but the pain in his heart hurt more.

No, this couldn't be happening. He couldn't lose Rachel. Not now. Not when he'd finally found himself and the Lord again.

He dropped to his knees, right there in the middle of the laundry room where no one could see his pain. Leaning against the washer, he bowed his head. As he closed his eyes, hot tears ran down his cheeks. And then, he prayed for the second time that night. He asked forgiveness for turning his back on the Lord and he begged for help. And when he finished talking to his Heavenly Father, a feeling of peace settled over him. He didn't know what the future held for him and Rachel, but he knew they had to be together. He couldn't give up on them. He must convince her that he loved her more than he loved his own life. Somehow he'd find a way to win Danny over.

Standing, he walked into the kitchen, his legs numb from kneeling so long. He wasn't too old for Rachel. Not when his love made him feel so young and free.

He'd go see them first thing in the morning and tell them that he loved them and wanted to share his life with them. Somehow, he'd make both Rachel and Danny see they were good together. That they could build a happy life here in Finnegan's Valley. That they could be a forever family.

Chapter Seventeen

In the morning, Rachel prepared oatmeal with raisins and brown sugar for Gladys and the boys. The children scooped the food into their mouths, and both seemed like their old selves as they chased Stripe around the house.

Gladys smiled as she helped clear the table. "It's nothing short of a miracle. We have a lot to celebrate."

"Yes, we've been truly blessed."

Shortly afterward, Gladys took Charlie home. Rachel was preparing to take Danny into town to deposit Grammy's money and then over to visit Sam when she heard the sounds of a car outside.

Danny knelt on the sofa, pulling aside the curtains so he could stare out the window. "It's Sam. He's all dressed up, like he's going to church or something."

Rachel gasped. Good thing she'd fixed her hair and put on her makeup. "Danny, come away from there. It's not polite to stare."

He did as told, padding over to her in his slippers. "What does he want now?"

"I think he wants to be a part of our family."

"Why can't he get his own family?" he grumbled.

"Because he doesn't want another family. He loves us." Sam hadn't really said the words, but she knew he loved them.

Danny's forehead creased. "Do you love him, too?"

"Yes, I do. Very much. What do you think?"

He hesitated, his mouth puckered in a scowl.

"You know, Sam's been very good to us. And he's never asked anything in return."

"Yeah, he's okay I guess. But—"

She caught the sound of a car door slamming. "Let's talk more about this later. Right now, I'd appreciate it if you'd be nice. Why don't you go work on your new airplane model and give me time to speak with Sam alone?"

He frowned but went obediently to his bedroom.

She opened the door and stepped out on the porch before Sam even made it through the front gate. Her pulse kicked into double-time. Seeing him brought her a feeling of peace, like being set free after spending a year in prison.

He wore his best pair of shiny cowboy boots, and gray dress slacks. He wore his coats unbuttoned and she saw a starched white shirt and bolo tie with a large ornamental slide made of polished turquoise. His inky black hair had been combed back and caught the rays of morning sunshine. She thought him the most handsome man in the world.

As he opened the gate to her white picket fence and stepped inside the yard, Shadow rushed toward her. Rachel didn't think before she reacted. Lifting one hand, she pointed at the ground and spoke with command. "Sit!"

The black Lab sat and licked his chops while Rachel took a deep breath and released it. She'd done it! She'd learned how to deal with dogs. Now, if she could tell Sam how she felt.

"What are you doing here?" Oh, couldn't she do better than that? What she really wanted to say was—

"I came to see you and Danny." His eyes sparkled with a smile as he sauntered toward her, all tall muscular strength.

She lifted her brows. "You sure look nice. Any special occasion?"

"Yes, I have something important I want to say to you."

Her heart turned into a roller coaster. "And I want to tell you something, too."

He followed her inside and tossed his jacket and best felt hat onto the sofa.

"Won't you sit down?" she asked.

"No, I'll stand, thanks. But I think we should include Danny in our conversation. I don't want to cause him any more sadness or do anything he won't agree to."

His consideration didn't surprise her. He'd always put other people's needs first. "Okay, let me get him."

She walked down the hall and opened the door to Danny's bedroom. "Danny, Sam's here to see both of us."

The empty room stared back at her, the window open wide. Lying on the floor were Danny's Rocketman jammies. She picked them up—

Oh, no!

"Danny!" she called, racing to the bathroom to see if he was there. His coat and boots were missing and she ran back to the living room. "He's gone."

"What do you mean?" Sam's eyes narrowed.

She grabbed her coat and jerked open the front door. "I think he's run away."

Sam followed her outside, thrusting his arms into his jacket. On the porch, he reached out and squeezed her arm. "Don't worry, we'll find him. Where do you think he went?"

His reassurance helped. Surely Danny wouldn't be foolish enough to cross the ice again—

"He couldn't have gone far. This way."

Fear caused her to quicken her step. As she circled the house, Sam followed, their feet crunching through the snow. Rachel scanned the pond, half-grateful and half-fearful when she saw no sign of her son. She hurried on, breathing in and out.

"He must have gone over to your place." She fought against the stitch in her side.

"He must really hate me."

"No, I think he's just confused." She tried to hide the fear in her voice, the trembling of her body. What if Danny caught another chill and became seriously ill?

She fought to keep up with Sam's long strides. He moved ahead, his face drawn with determination. "Don't worry, Rachel. We'll find him."

The cold seeped into her bones as they slogged through the melting snow. "It's dangerous out here for a little boy."

"He's going to be all right. There!" Sam pointed at small footprints heading toward his place.

They followed in hot pursuit. Twenty minutes later, they reached Sam's driveway. Rachel's heart thundered in her ears and her breath came in rapid bursts.

"I think I know where he's gone." Sam loped over to the barn, then opened one of the double doors. Rachel followed. Inside, she caught the sweet scent of fresh hay, leather and animals. She blinked, letting her eyes adjust to the dim interior.

In the farthest stall, Danny sat cuddled back in the straw with his puppy. Sam had found homes for the other litter-mates. Rachel pressed a hand to her chest, breathless with relief. Danny had gone where he felt happy and safe. She'd brought him to Finley for the very same reasons.

The boy clutched Blackie in his arms. When he saw them, Danny stared at Sam with wide, fearful eyes. "Go away and leave me alone. I don't want another father. I'm the man of the house now. Not you."

Sam's face drained of color. "Is that why you ran away? You think I'm trying to take your daddy's place?"

Danny nodded, his eyes filled with tears, his nose crinkled like he might cry. "I like you, Sam, but he's my daddy. What if I forget him?"

"We could never forget your father." Rachel lifted the latch on the gate so she could step inside the stall. Sam followed, standing back, giving them space.

"But if I love Sam, Daddy might think I don't love him anymore."

As Rachel sat beside her son in the straw, he cringed, refusing to look at her, holding Blackie tighter.

Losing his father and all the contention since that time had taken its toll on the boy. She had no intention of taking his dog from him. Danny was entitled to some happiness.

"Is that why you don't want another father? Because you're afraid Daddy might think you don't love him?"

Danny nodded, not meeting her eyes.

"That's not true. Daddy knows you'll love him forever."

The puppy squirmed free of Danny's arms and jumped up on her, licking her face. It didn't bother her like it used to and she chuckled, marveling at how she'd outgrown her fear of dogs.

Well, most dogs.

She reached over and scratched Blackie's ears. The puppy yawned, its pink tongue curling back in its little chops. The dog nudged Rachel's hand with its nose.

"Danny, would you mind if we took Blackie over to our place to live with us?" Rachel asked.

A thatch of hair fell over Danny's forehead and his face lit up with a smile. Rachel smoothed his hair back with her fingertips. "You mean it, Mom? We can really keep her?"

Her gaze met Sam's and she caught his smile of approval. "If it's okay with Sam."

The man crouched beside Danny as the dog covered the boy's face with puppy kisses. "Of course. Blackie needs a family of her own. She's all alone now."

Danny looked at Sam and dawning filled his eyes. "She's alone, just like you."

Sam nodded. "She doesn't want anything from you. She just wants to love you. I feel the same way. I just want to love you. I don't want to take your daddy's place."

The child looked at his mother, his eyes filled with tears. "I wanted us to be a family, but I was afraid."

"Of what?" Rachel asked.

"Of hurting Daddy's feelings."

"Oh, Danny! Daddy would want you to be happy. It's gonna be okay. You don't need to be afraid anymore."

Sam rested a hand on the boy's shoulder. "I'd be disappointed if you didn't remember and love your father. But do you think you can accept me, too?"

Danny heaved a shuddering sigh before nodding. "Yeah, I want Mommy to be happy. And I know she loves you as much as she loved my dad."

Draping one arm around Danny's shoulders, Rachel leaned down and kissed the top of his head. He smelled of puppy breath. She picked up Blackie and placed the dog in her son's lap. "Happy birthday."

"Thanks, Mom!" Danny threw one arm around her neck. "I promise to take good care of Blackie."

Tears burned Rachel's eyes. When he drew back, her son looked just like Alex. Strong and in control. Prepared to always do what was right. She couldn't fault him for being loyal to his father. She wouldn't have it any other way.

She looked at Sam and his eyes spoke volumes as he

nodded his head. "Let's go in the house where it's warm. Why don't you bring Blackie with you?"

Sam helped Rachel stand. Danny cradled Blackie in his arms, as they all walked through the gate together.

Minutes later, Danny sat at the kitchen table, one hand wrapped around a mug of hot chocolate as he worked a jigsaw puzzle. The puppy lay at his feet, chewing on his shoelaces.

Rachel stood in the living room with Sam, reticent to leave Danny alone for even a moment.

Sam jutted his chin toward the boy. "You really think he can accept me?"

"He already has. He's always liked you, Sam. Now, he gets to love you like a father." She reached out and adjusted the turquoise slide on his bolo tie before smoothing the palm of her hand across his chest. "Thanks for fixing my rocking chair."

"You're welcome. I knew it meant a lot to you."

"Now it means even more."

He reached up and caught her hand, staring into her eyes.

She smiled. "And thanks for finding Grammy's bank account. Who would have believed she had it hidden beneath the floorboards?"

He didn't laugh. "Are you serious about staying here in Finley?"

"Of course. Why?"

He shrugged, his eyes crinkling. "I thought you might leave, now you have the resources to go wherever you want."

"No. I'm staying right here where I belong." She took a step nearer, closing the space between them.

His breathing accelerated. "Stop it."

"What?" She cupped his cheek with her hand.

He turned his head away, his eyes closing for just a moment, as if he couldn't believe she would touch him like this. "Stop teasing me. Stop looking at me like that."

"Like what?"

"Like you love me."

"But I do."

He stared. "You do?"

"Uh-huh." She beamed, happier than she'd been in a long time.

He smiled and breathed a huge sigh of relief. "I'm sure glad. Because I want to get you a new mailbox."

"A new mailbox?"

"Yeah, one with a new last name and my address on it. I'm in love with you. And it's pretty rotten to love someone who doesn't love you back. Believe me, I know."

She laughed. "Well, rest assured that I love you very much. After you left us last night, I realized how much. I was so worried about Danny accepting you. I planned to come over here and apologize and tell you how much I want you in my life."

"You do?"

"Yes," she said, her heart filled with bliss.

He pulled her into his arms and held her tight, his lips moving against her hair. "I'm so glad. I dressed up to come over to your house this morning and ask for a second chance at love. I probably don't deserve it, but I realized I'd left my heart with you and I couldn't see straight or feel anything until you said you loved me, too."

Butterflies fluttered inside her stomach. She thought she'd never hear anyone say such things to her again. "Yes, Sam. I love you."

"I can't tell you how glad I am to hear you say that." He brushed his lips close to her ear. "Stay with me always. I'm crazy about both you and Danny. He's a great kid and I want us to be a family. Be my wife, Rachel. Be the love of my life."

"Hey! Are you gonna marry Sam?"

They broke apart and stared at Danny, who stood in the doorway watching them.

So much for romantic privacy. But what could you expect with a seven-year-old bouncing around the house? Rachel stared at her son, wondering at his reaction to her marrying Sam. Then, she decided it would be best to get it out in the open right now. "Yes, I've agreed to marry Sam."

"Hooray! We're gonna get married and eat cake." Danny picked up Blackie and swung the puppy around in a little dance.

"Hey, come here, lady." Sam pulled Rachel behind the bookcase and into his arms where they wouldn't be observed by prying eyes. She giggled, her heart so light she thought she could fly.

Reaching into his front pants pocket, Sam went down on one knee as he took her left hand in his. "I want to do this properly. I love you, Rachel. More than words can say. Marry me and stay with me always. Never leave me lonely again."

Tears washed her cheeks, but she didn't bother to brush them away. "You're sure this is what you want?"

"If you love me, I am."

"I do, Sam. I love you. So very much."

He smiled tenderly, showing that endearing dimple in his cheek as he slid the ring onto her fourth finger. "This was my mother's wedding ring. I'd be pleased if you'd wear it until we can drive to a town with a jewelry store where I can buy you your own ring."

"I think this one will do just fine." She stared at the simple beauty of the small diamond and dainty setting. "It's lovely. Do you make a habit of carrying this with you?"

"Just when I'm about to propose marriage."

She laughed, hardly able to believe how her life had worked out. The Lord had truly mended their broken hearts.

As Sam took her into his arms, she realized this was where she belonged. Sheltered in his arms and God's redeeming love. Always and forever.

* * * * *

Dear Reader,

Have you ever said something you regretted? Maybe you didn't really mean it, but you were angry, upset or hurt, and out it came. So fast you couldn't grab it back. And then the damage was done. Maybe you apologized, but it was too late. It was embedded in someone's heart and mind. Someone you cared for deeply. You could spend the rest of your life never saying it again, working to prove you didn't really mean it. But nothing you could say or do would ever fix it. You had said it, and only one thing could ever make it right: their forgiveness.

In *The Forever Family*, the hero is haunted by his cruel words to his fiancée, just before she died. He never got the chance to apologize and make things right with her. His remorse was great and he blamed himself and the Lord for her death. We never fully know the harm our words might cause. Thoughtless or intentional, our words can cut deeper than any knife. Our loved ones often bear the brunt of our sharp tongues.

According to the *Gospel of John*, when He walked the earth, the Savior gave us a new commandment to love one another. In this day and age, we need this directive more than ever. I am convinced if we offered expressions of love and appreciation instead of anger and condemnation, our families would be happier, and the world a less contentious place in which to live.

I hope you enjoy reading The Forever Family, and I invite you to visit my Web site at www.LeighBale.com to learn more about my books.

May you find peace in the Lord's words!
Leigh Bale

QUESTIONS FOR DISCUSSION

1. In *The Forever Family*, Rachel felt guilty for asking God to help her overcome her phobia of dogs. Do you think her prayer is insignificant? Have you ever felt the need to ask God for help with something that might seem small and unimportant to others?

2. Rachel's rocking chair serves as a symbol in the story. Why did it mean so much to her? Why did it come to mean even more to her later on?

3. Grief is part of the healing process. Why did Rachel feel disloyal to her deceased husband for having deep feelings for Sam?

4. When people lose their spouse to death or divorce, is it okay for them to move on into another loving relationship? Why or why not?

5. Danny mourned his father and feared Sam might try to take his father's place. How did Rachel comfort Danny? Have you ever dealt with a child's grief over losing a parent? How did you help reassure that child?

6. Have you ever mourned a loved one? How did you find the strength to move on and find joy in your life?

7. We each have grief in our lives. How can the Atonement of Christ swallow our pain and bring us peace and joy?

8. What opportunities have you had to bear someone else's burdens? How can we mourn with those who mourn?

How has someone else mourned with you and helped you bear your burdens?

9. Sam's last words to his fiancée were cruel and biting. Have you ever said something mean to a person whom you care about? Did you later regret what you said? What steps might you take to make this right? How can we help prevent ourselves from letting this happen again? And how can we take negative feelings of guilt and make them a positive experience for our good?

10. After Sam's fiancée died, he blamed God for her death. Was God responsible? Why or why not?

11. Why was it so difficult for Sam to pray? Why do some people blame God when tragedy strikes while others are able to see His hand working for good in their lives?

12. In the story, Danny mistook a complete stranger for his deceased father. Do you believe children grieve the same way adults do? How might their grief differ from an adult's grief?

13. How can we prepare our children so that when tragedy strikes, the child is not left devastated? Likewise, how can we prepare our children so they see the hand of the Lord in their lives even when tragedy strikes?

A thrilling romance between a British nurse
and an American cowboy on the African plains.

Turn the page for a sneak preview of
THE MAVERICK'S BRIDE
by Catherine Palmer.
Available September 2009
from Love Inspired® Historical.

Adam hoisted himself onto the balcony, swinging one leg at a time over the rail. He hoped he hadn't been spotted by a compound guard.

But the sight of Emma Pickering peering out from behind the curtain put his concerns to rest. He had done the right thing.

"Good morning, Miss Pickering." He leaned against the white window frame.

"Mr. King." She was almost breathless. "I cannot speak with you."

"But I need to talk. Mind if I come inside?"

"Indeed, sir, you may not take another step! Are you mad?"

He couldn't hold back a grin. "No more than most. I figure anyone who would leave home and travel all the way to Africa has to be a little off-kilter."

"You refer to me, I suppose? I'll have you know I'm here for a very good reason."

"Railway inspection, is it? Or nursing?"

Emma looked even better than he had thought she might—and he had thought about her a lot.

"Speaking of nursing," he ventured.

"Mr. King, I have already told you I'm unavailable. Now please let yourself down by that…that rope thing, and—"

"My lasso?"

"You must go down again, sir. This is unseemly."

Emma was edgy this morning. Almost frightened. Different from the bold young woman he had met yesterday.

He couldn't let that concern him. Last night after he left the consulate, he had made up his mind to keep things strictly business with Emma Pickering.

"I'll leave after I've had my say," he told her. "This is important."

"Speak quickly, sir. My father must not find you here."

"With all due respect, Emma, do you think I'm concerned about what your father thinks?"

"You may not care, but I do. What do you want from me?"

"I need a nurse."

"A nurse? Are you ill?"

"Not for me. I have a friend—at my ranch."

Her eyes deepened in concern as she let the curtain drop a little. "What sort of illness does your friend have? Can you describe it?"

Adam looked away. How could he explain the situation without scaring her off?

"It's not an illness. It's more like…"

Searching for the right words, he turned back to Emma. But at the first full sight of her face, he reached through the open window and pulled the curtain out of her hands.

"Emma, what happened to you?" He caught her arm and drew her toward him. "Who did this?"

She raised her hand in a vain effort to cover her cheek and eye. "It's nothing," she protested, trying to back away. "Please, Mr. King, you must not…"

Even as she tried to speak, he stepped through the balcony door and gathered her into his arms. Brushing back the hair from her cheek, he noted the swelling and the darkening stain around it.

"Emma," he growled. "Who did this to you?"

She fell motionless, silent in his embrace. No wonder she had shied like a scared colt. She hadn't wanted him to know.

Torn with dismay that anyone would ever harm this beautiful woman, he felt an irresistible urge to kiss her.

"Emma, you have to tell me...." Realization flooded through him. A pompous, nattily dressed English railroad tycoon had struck his own daughter.

"Leave me, I beg you. You have no place here."

"Emma, wait. Listen to me." Adam caught her wrists and pulled her back toward him. He'd never been a man to think things through too carefully. He did what felt right.

"I want you to come with me," he told her. "I need your help. Let's go right now. Emma, I'll take care of you."

"I don't need anyone to take care of me," she shot back. "God is watching over me."

"Emma!" Both turned toward the open door where Emma's sister stood, eyes wide.

"Emma, go with him!" Cissy crossed the room toward them. "Run away with him, Emma. It's your chance to escape—to become a nurse, as you've always wanted. You'll be safe at last, and you can have your dream."

Emma turned back to Adam.

"Come on," he urged her. "Let's get moving."

* * * * *

*Will Emma run away with Adam and finally realize her
dreams of becoming a nurse?
Find out in THE MAVERICK'S BRIDE,
available in September 2009 only from
Love Inspired® Historical.*

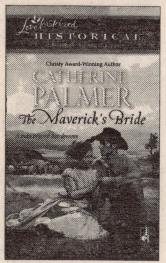

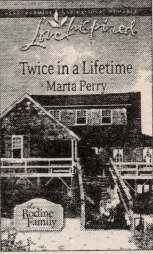

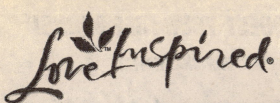

Take one uncontrollable little girl. Add a home infested with bees. Toss in former childhood nemesis Anna Burdett, and what single dad Reeves Leland gets is one big headache! But could this reunion spark old memories and new possibilities for a future together?

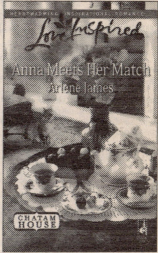

Look for

Anna Meets Her Match

by
Arlene James

Available September 2009 wherever books are sold.

www.SteepleHill.com

REQUEST YOUR FREE BOOKS!

2 FREE INSPIRATIONAL NOVELS
PLUS 2
FREE
MYSTERY GIFTS

YES! Please send me 2 FREE Love Inspired® novels and my 2 FREE mystery gifts (gifts are worth about $10). After receiving them, if I don't wish to receive any more books, I can return the shipping statement marked "cancel". If I don't cancel, I will receive 4 brand-new novels every month and be billed just $4.24 per book in the U.S. or $4.74 per book in Canada. That's a savings of over 20% off the cover price. It's quite a bargain! Shipping and handling is just 50¢ per book.* I understand that accepting the 2 free books and gifts places me under no obligation to buy anything. I can always return a shipment and cancel at any time. Even if I never buy another book, the two free books and gifts are mine to keep forever.

113 IDN EYK2   313 IDN EYLE

Name	(PLEASE PRINT)	
Address		Apt. #
City	State/Prov.	Zip/Postal Code

Signature (if under 18, a parent or guardian must sign)

Mail to Steeple Hill Reader Service:
IN U.S.A.: P.O. Box 1867, Buffalo, NY 14240-1867
IN CANADA: P.O. Box 609, Fort Erie, Ontario L2A 5X3

Not valid to current subscribers of Love Inspired books.

Want to try two free books from another series?
Call 1-800-873-8635 or visit www.morefreebooks.com

* Terms and prices subject to change without notice. Prices do not include applicable taxes. Sales tax applicable in N.Y. Canadian residents will be charged applicable provincial taxes and GST. Offer not valid in Quebec. This offer is limited to one order per household. All orders subject to approval. Credit or debit balances in a customer's account(s) may be offset by any other outstanding balance owed by or to the customer. Please allow 4 to 6 weeks for delivery. Offer available while quantities last.

Your Privacy: Steeple Hill Books is committed to protecting your privacy. Our Privacy Policy is available online at www.SteepleHill.com or upon request from the Reader Service. From time to time we make our lists of customers available to reputable third parties who may have a product or service of interest to you. If you would prefer we not share your name and address, please check here. ☐

LIREG09

Love Inspired™

TITLES AVAILABLE NEXT MONTH
Available August 25, 2009

TWICE IN A LIFETIME by Marta Perry
The Bodine Family

Brokenhearted Georgia Lee Bodine didn't want lawyer Matthew Harper
poking around her family history, even if that's why her grandmother
hired him. Matthew's equally damaged but caring heart makes Georgia
reconsider, and open *her* heart to a second chance at love.

REKINDLED HEARTS by Brenda Minton
After the Storm

When a tornado traps Lexi Harmon and her ex-husband together,
she prays they have a second chance. And as they work together to
rebuild the town, she works on rebuilding their love—one piece
of his heart at a time.

ANNA MEETS HER MATCH by Arlene James
Chatam House

Take one uncontrollable little girl. Add a home infested with bees.
Toss in former childhood nemesis Anna Burdett, and what single dad
Reeves Leland gets is one big headache! But could this reunion spark
old memories and new possibilities for a future together?

DAD IN TRAINING by Gail Gaymer Martin

Special needs teacher Molly Manning thinks a dog is just what workaholic
Brent Runyan needs to reach his troubled nephew. After all, if Brent
can open his heart to a loving canine, maybe he'll find room in it for
Molly as well.

A TEXAS RANGER'S FAMILY by Mae Nunn

Home with the husband and child she abandoned years ago is the
last place photographer Erin Grey wants to be. But Texas Ranger Daniel
is ready to prove that her love is something he never gave up on.

HOMETOWN REUNION by Pam Andrews

Single father Scott Mara is busy renovating the town café. But
Lori Raymond still remembers him as the high school bad boy
who stole her heart. Can he show her that he may be a changed man
but his love for Lori remains the same?

LICNMBPA0809